"Something wrong?" Zac turned to look at her.

That's when Libby made her mistake. She met his gaze head-on, and when she saw the hunger displayed so blatantly in his eyes, she was lost. How could she fight the unfightable, stop the unstoppable? She sighed and surrendered gracefully to fate.

Zac laced his fingers through her hair, lowered his head to hers, and kissed each corner of her mouth. He kissed the tip of her nose, her eyelids, and pressed a trail of kisses along her jaw. But he didn't take her lips until Libby wove her hands through his hair and opened her mouth to his.

With a groan he pulled her closer, his hands caressing her body with surprising heat. Libby closed her eyes. She'd tried not to want this, but she'd never wanted anything more. And more than anything she wanted to touch him.

Zac seemed to know what she wanted as her hands opened his shirt and began to roam over his broad, muscled chest. Placing his hand on hers, he pressed it to him. "Feel my heart beat, Libby. Feel it race." She looked up at him wordlessly, all the need shining in her eyes, and he whispered, "Show me how you want me to touch you. . . ."

WHAT ARE *LOVESWEPT* ROMANCES?

They are stories of true romance and touching emotion. We believe those two very important ingredients are constants in our highly sensual and very believable stories in the LOVESWEPT line. Our goal is to give you, the reader, stories of consistently high quality that may sometimes make you laugh, sometimes make you cry, but are always fresh and creative and contain many delightful surprises within their pages.

Most romance fans read an enormous number of books. Those they truly love, they keep. Others may be traded with friends and soon forgotten. We hope that each LOVESWEPT romance will be a treasure—a "keeper." We will always try to publish

LOVE STORIES YOU'LL NEVER FORGET
BY AUTHORS YOU'LL ALWAYS REMEMBER

The Editors

THEN COMES MARRIAGE

BONNIE
PEGA

BANTAM BOOKS

NEW YORK · TORONTO · LONDON · SYDNEY · AUCKLAND

THEN COMES MARRIAGE
A Bantam Book / July 1993

If you would be interested in receiving protective vinyl covers for your
Loveswept books, please write to this address for information:

> Loveswept
> Bantam Books
> P.O. Box 985
> Hicksville, NY 11802

ISBN 0-553-44405-0

Published simultaneously in the United States and Canada

Bantam Books are published by Bantam Books, a division of Bantam Dou-
bleday Dell Publishing Group, Inc. Its trademark, consisting of the words
"Bantam Books" and the portrayal of a rooster, is Registered in U.S. Patent
and Trademark Office and in other countries. Marca Registrada. Bantam
Books, 1540 Broadway, New York, New York 10036.

PRINTED IN THE UNITED STATES OF AMERICA

OPM   0 9 8 7 6 5 4 3 2 1

Special thanks to Lamaze instructor
Nina Blodgett for answering
my questions.

This book is dedicated with love
to the memory of my own role models
for a happy marriage—my parents,
Luther and Ila Martin.

ONE

Liberty Austin couldn't help but notice the man who'd just walked in the door. He looked like he'd rather be anywhere but there.

"You okay?"

She smiled at her best friend and labor coach, Deb Greenley, and whispered, "I'm fine, Deb, but"—she affectionately patted her swollen abdomen—"Cupcake here is getting restless." She turned her curious gaze back to the man standing in the entrance. "Do you know him?"

"Nooo, but he *is* good to look at, don't you think?"

Libby gave a noncommittal shrug, but privately agreed. He was a few inches over six feet and about two hundred pounds, and he filled up the doorway as though he were a giant. And his size had nothing to do with it—it was the self-confidence he exuded.

She couldn't tell what color his eyes were, but they were fringed with startlingly long dark lashes that might have made him look effeminate if his features weren't so rugged. His lips were thin and sensual and currently curled in an uncomfortable smile as he murmured something to the very pregnant blonde at his side.

Libby suppressed a sigh. She should have figured he was married. Single men seldom frequented Lamaze classes. Not that she needed another man in her life, she mused as she absently rubbed her side where a small elbow or knee prodded her. After all, she was still dealing with the aftereffects of the last man in her life.

After four miserable years of marriage, she'd been left with the house, a stack of bills the size of the national debt, and Cupcake. Bobby, on the other hand, had absconded to Nassau with his nineteen-year-old secretary. Yet Libby felt like she'd gotten the better deal. Despite her occasional bouts of insecurity over the prospect of raising a child alone, she was still far happier now than she'd been in a long time.

"They showed up just in time for break." Deb grinned as Mabel, the Lamaze teacher, indicated juice and decaffeinated coffee in the corner.

Libby got to her feet as gracefully as twenty-six extra pounds would allow, and followed Deb to the refreshments. "He looks like he'd rather not have shown up at all," she murmured.

"Definitely a fish out of water," agreed Deb.

A fish indeed. Libby had been fishing a couple of times in her life and she knew that there were the ones you threw back and the ones that were keepers. He looked like a keeper to her.

Zachary Webster surveyed the room of pregnant women and sighed. He'd rather have been diving into a pool of sharks. Or entering a room full of the hungry corporate variety—he knew what to do there. He did it every day. Here, he just felt like a beached whale—flopping around futilely on the sand.

He looked around the room again, his eyes alighting on a dark-haired woman with the porcelain complexion and tranquil countenance of a Madonna. He took in too many things about her to absorb them all at once—sleek, shiny hair that swung down her back, the lushness of her breasts, the delicate rounded curve of her cheek, the not-so-delicate rounded curve of her abdomen. Damn.

"Are you going to stand there all day, or are you going in?"

Zac pulled his attention away from the mesmerizing woman and smiled affectionately at his sister-in-law. "You owe me for this, Hannah. You really do."

She smiled back and hooked her arm through his. "You'll live, Zac m'dear."

"Ben should have been here with you," Zac muttered. "He has no business—"

"Well, he's not here," Hannah interrupted. "And you are."

"Lucky me." He found his gaze again lingering on the Madonna. Silk and satin, he thought. Skin that looked silky-soft, hair with the sleek sheen of satin. Definitely the kind of woman who would be heaven to hold—and hell on his plans.

When the break was over, they joined the other couples on the floor. The Lamaze instructor turned out the lights and began showing a film of a natural childbirth. As they watched the woman on the screen go through labor, Zac heard a feminine voice mutter, "I wonder if it's too late to change my mind and go to the nearest cabbage patch instead." Terrific voice, he thought, sexy-soft and laced with humor.

He turned his head to see who'd made the remark, which he could wholeheartedly endorse, and met the dark blue eyes of his Madonna. Only they weren't Madonna eyes. The merry sparkle belied the cool serenity of her face.

When she saw his look, she gave a sheepish smile and shrugged.

He caught his breath. Her lips looked as soft and pink as the blush on a ripe peach, and they were parted slightly in a delectable smile. It seemed to crawl inside him and heat him clear through. He had to meet her.

"I'm Zac Webster," he whispered. "And this is Hannah."

Hannah turned around. "Hi," she said.

"I'm Liberty Austen. Libby. And this is my labor coach, Deb Greenley."

Hannah winked at the other two women and said, "Zac's brother said that when Zac was thirteen, he threw up when his gerbil had babies. How I'm ever going to get him into the delivery room, I don't know."

Deb piped up, "How about a whip and a chair?" The three women smiled companionably.

"Don't you think you should watch the film and quit picking on me?" asked Zac.

"Maybe *you* should watch the film," Hannah countered. "You might learn something."

"That's what I'm afraid of," Zac muttered, and turned back to the film.

Zac was a nice name, Libby thought wistfully,

her eyes lingering on the back of his head. His dark hair looked as though it had been expertly cut and styled, yet unruly waves still gave his hair the appearance of having had impatient fingers run through it—or maybe a woman's fingers. She wondered if it was as soft as it looked, then frowned at the sudden urge to touch it and find out.

She squirmed, feeling uncomfortable about thinking about one man while carrying another man's baby. Even though she and Bobby were divorced—and it had been over between them long before that—it felt like cheating.

She pulled her attention to the film, which showed a tired, perspiring, but obviously elated couple cooing over the brand-new baby in their arms. Libby fought back a sharp stab of envy, and her eyes burned with tears. She'd have given anything to be able to share the birth of her baby with someone who loved her. She didn't even want to think about all the other things she wouldn't be able to share—the first tooth, the first word, the first step. Libby set her jaw and willed the always-looming loneliness away.

When class was over, a group of couples decided to go to the ice cream shop next door. Deb excused herself, since she had to be at the office early the next day, but Libby, always in the mood for ice cream—especially chocolate—went and found herself sharing a booth with Zac and Hannah.

The two women hit it off with the instant camaraderie that can occur only between two women going through the eighth month of pregnancy at the same time. They compared notes on doctors, baby names, and swollen ankles, discussed the virtues of breastfeeding over bottle feeding and compared brands of diapers.

And somehow, in between all the pleasant chatter, Hannah managed to ferret out all kinds of information about Libby. She found out Libby was divorced, a junior high school teacher, had a house not more than a couple of miles from Hannah's, loved football, baseball, and art exhibits, and was allergic to strawberries.

Zac watched his sister-in-law with amazement, tinged with a great deal of respect. Perry Mason couldn't have learned so much about Libby. And the tidbits she was uncovering about the intriguing woman with the Madonna smile and hellion eyes interested him. For some reason, he felt both relieved and angry to learn she was divorced. He was angry because she had to go through her baby's birth alone. He felt relieved because— well, he shied away from thinking about that.

Funny, he liked football and baseball and art

exhibits too. He wasn't allergic to strawberries but didn't like them very much. As Hannah continued her sleuthing, he found out that Libby loved old movies and read both science fiction and murder mysteries. So did he. He sighed. Just his luck to have to have so much in common with a woman who was eight months pregnant.

"You and Zac certainly have a lot in common," remarked Hannah as if echoing his thoughts. "Oh, did you know Tyler's is having a sale on infants' clothes Saturday? Do you want to meet for lunch and go check it out?"

"I'd love to," said Libby. She licked a last bit of chocolate from her spoon.

"Then I'll call you Friday night to arrange a time. Zac, it's after ten. You said you had an early meeting tomorrow and you still have to take me home. Libby, where are you parked?"

"Just around the corner." Libby eyed the two of them speculatively. Take Hannah home first? Were they married or weren't they? Hannah wore a ring. Zac didn't, but then, some men didn't. Maybe they were divorced or separated.

Libby felt better at that thought. She liked Hannah a lot and had been feeling more than a little guilty at finding another woman's husband so attractive. She was surprised she'd reacted so strongly to Zac. She wasn't feeling exactly sexy these days. She felt too isolated, scared, and exhausted. And fat.

After opening the door to his car and seating Hannah, Zac offered to walk Libby to her car. He cupped a hand under her elbow and headed in the direction she indicated.

When Zac turned the corner and saw an ancient, dilapidated old Volkswagen, he paused. "Is *that* your car?"

Libby stopped to dig her keys out of her purse, then turned and smiled at Zac. "Is something wrong?"

"You can't drive that."

"Why not?" she asked defensively. "She's a perfectly wonderful car."

"She?"

"Martha."

"You named your car?"

"What's wrong with that?"

"Uh, nothing. It's great. Terrific." He looked from her well-rounded stomach to the front seat of the small car. How in the world did she ever fit in there? Of course, even eight months along, she looked willowy and delicate of build. He found himself wondering how she'd feel in his arms. Would she feel dainty and fragile or lithe and strong? He hurriedly chased those thoughts away.

Fantasizing about a pregnant woman was just this side of weird.

"Thanks for walking me to my car." Libby opened her door and squeezed in. She turned the key and the engine came to life—complaining and wheezing all the way.

"You sure that thing's going to make it home?"

"She just needs a tuneup," Libby said, absently brushing a strand of hair from her face. Something about Zac, especially when he towered over her as he did then, made her feel delicate and feminine. She rather enjoyed the feeling too. It had been several months since she'd felt anything but ungainly.

"It needs a lot more than that. Why don't you retire it?" Zac leaned casually against the side of the car.

"She and I have been through a lot together. She was the first car I ever had. I bought her from Dad."

"Was it the traditional 'only got driven to church on Sunday?'"

Libby grinned. "Considering my father's a minister, that's more on the nose than you know."

That grin did strange things to his insides. He'd thought her smile was disturbing. That grin was more so. It made him want to tickle her to see if she giggled, to kiss her to see how it tasted. Only he couldn't afford to feel that way. It didn't fit in his plans. And his plans were everything; they hadn't let him down yet. The smartest thing to do would be to leave before he said or did something stupid.

"Good night." Zac turned abruptly and walked away, leaving Libby staring after him in bewilderment.

Libby and Deb arrived late at the next class. When they walked in, the class was already involved in practicing relaxation techniques. Libby looked for a seat in the back, but Hannah waved them over.

"I was afraid you weren't coming," Hannah whispered.

"My car died," Libby whispered back.

"I knew it!" Zac muttered. "I knew that it was only a matter of time before that deathtrap-on-wheels quit on you. With a baby coming, you need to think about a more reliable automobile. Have you thought about looking at the new . . . ?"

Libby tuned out his words, listening instead to his voice. It was the perfect combination of rough and soft—like the roughness of a man's whiskers over the smooth, warm skin beneath. It was a terrific voice for whispering words of love and passion to a woman—or for talking nonsense to a baby.

She called a halt to her wayward thoughts. She shouldn't be thinking things like that, not about Hannah's . . . Hannah's what? Ex-husband? If he was Hannah's ex, then Hannah obviously didn't feel the least bit possessive, judging from the way she'd mentioned more than once how much Libby and Zac had in common.

But it wasn't so much what they had in common that disturbed Libby. It was that he made her acutely aware of not having had a man's arms around her in months. Her breasts were so sensitive these days. She wondered how they'd feel crushed against a man's chest—his chest.

Libby forced herself to concentrate as the instructor talked about breathing. When it came time to practice, Zac glanced at her, and she managed a weak smile, wishing he'd look somewhere else. She felt like a complete fool going, "hee-hee-hee-hoo" with him watching. When he looked at her, she had enough trouble breathing at all.

Their breathing session was interrupted by an electronic beep from Deb's purse. Deb smiled sheepishly and slipped to the phone in the corner of the room. A minute later she was back. "I've got to go. I have a sixteen-year-old patient who got one of his bicuspids knocked out in a baseball game. This is what you get for having a dentist for a labor coach," she said ruefully. "I'll drop you off on the way to Mercy."

Libby shook her head. "You know darn well I'm twenty minutes or more out of the way. You go on to the hospital. I'll get home."

"Sure?"

"Sure. I'll call a cab."

"That won't be necessary," Hannah whispered over her shoulder. "Zac and I will see that you get home."

"Oh, no, really, I'll just—"

"Terrific!" Deb beamed. "Thanks a lot. I'll call you later, Libby."

When Deb left, there were only a few minutes left in class, but they seemed endless to Libby. Especially when the instructor began talking about a position for making love that took the pressure off the abdomen. Libby swallowed and involuntarily looked at Zac, only to find that he was looking at her. She hurriedly turned her head and tried to appear nonchalant as she glanced around the room.

Meanwhile, the instructor went on to describe several other positions and Libby shifted uncomfortably, determined not to let Zac catch her looking at him again. *Oh, Mabel*, she pleaded silently, *for heaven's sake, please change the subject!*

As if Mabel had heard her plea, she went on to talk about something else. Orgasms. "A lot of women find they become even sexier during the last trimester of pregnancy because of the increased circulation in the genital area. Some women even say they become multiorgasmic."

Libby wanted to find a hole to crawl into. She was almost ready to fake an exit to the bathroom, when the instructor began talking about breathing again.

She didn't take in a word the instructor said, her attention fastened instead on Zac. She kept sneaking glances at him as he coached Hannah in her breathing during the final minutes of class. He was so sweet and patient with Hannah that Libby wanted to cry. She'd give anything to have someone like that with her during labor. Being around Zac was making her feel lonelier than ever.

She brooded about that on the way home. While Zac and Hannah talked about class, Libby sat quietly in the backseat. She was so deep in thought that she was caught off guard when Hannah twisted around in her seat and looked questioningly at her.

"What?"

"I said, didn't you tell me Saturday that you

were planning on going to the pre-Columbian art exhibit tomorrow or the next day?"

"Yes, I did. As a matter of fact, I figured I'd probably go tomorrow afternoon."

Hannah turned a triumphant smile to Zac. "See? I told you she was planning to go." She turned back to Libby. "Zac said he was thinking about going tomorrow afternoon, and I told him that the two of you should go together. Right, Zac?"

Zac nodded and politely offered to pick Libby up at one o'clock.

Libby murmured her consent. Hannah chattered blithely on, until Zac pulled up in front of her house.

"Oh, do you both want to come in for some coffee?" Hannah asked. "Decaf, of course."

"No, I have an early meeting."

"No, thanks."

Zac and Libby spoke at the same time. Hannah just smiled. "Okay, then, I'll see you next week, Libby. Talk to you later, Zac. Bye."

Libby laboriously climbed out of the pitlike backseat of Zac's sports car and into the front. "Thanks for giving me a ride home. I live just off Pendleton." She gave him brief directions.

"Where did you take your ailing car?" he asked as they drove off.

"Emerson's on Beech Road. Are you familiar with them?"

"No, but Beech is just a few blocks over from the museum. I can drop you off to get your car after the exhibit tomorrow," he said as he pulled up into her driveway.

She fumbled with the seat belt. "That would be nice, thank you." She tugged at the buckle, then looked up with a grimace. "How do you unfasten . . . ? Oh, I see." She released the belt and turned toward him at the same time he reached over. This plopped her left breast squarely in his hand.

Their surprised gazes met and held for a moment, then slowly he drew his hand away, brushing his fingers across her distended nipple as he did so.

"I—I'll pick you up at, uh, what time did we say?"

"One o'clock, I think," Libby mumbled as she hooked her fingers through her purse strap and opened the car door. "You don't need to see me in." As a matter of fact, it would be better for everyone if he didn't.

Zac reached out one hand and snared a strand of hair, rubbing it back and forth between his thumb and forefinger. "I've been wondering if it was as silky as it looks," he murmured. "It is." He let go the strand as if it suddenly burned. "I'll see you tomorrow."

Libby went inside, then turned and looked back at Zac, still waiting in her driveway. She waved and shut the door. Only then did she hear his car pull away. She leaned back against the door. What a disturbing man! He made her aware of herself as a woman in a way that she hadn't been recently—it was hard to feel feminine when one felt roughly the same size as a hippopotamus.

It was only a little after nine-thirty, but she showered and got ready for bed anyway. She grabbed a book and lay down next to Wells, her golden retriever. She smiled absently as she nudged the dog over. He seemed to take it as his right to sprawl over two-thirds of the bed. Zac would probably sleep like that, she found herself thinking. He looked like a man who needed room.

Any woman who slept with him would have to get by with just a few inches of bed. Of course, any woman who slept with Zac would have other compensations, like his gorgeous body and strong hands.

Libby took a deep breath and pushed those thoughts away—shocked at herself. Eight months pregnant and fantasizing about what Zac would be like in bed. After Bobby, she neither needed nor wanted another man in her life. The only good thing to come out of her disastrous four-year marriage was the baby. And that had been an accident.

A couple of days after she'd told Bobby about the pregnancy, he'd run off, leaving behind a note saying he was relinquishing all rights to the child. Not long after came quickie divorce papers in the mail from Nassau.

And now here she was eight months later, at the beginning of summer. With no classes to occupy her mind, she worried almost constantly about raising a child on her own. Was she capable of it? Could she support herself and a baby on a junior high school teacher's salary? Would her child be irreparably harmed by not having a male figure around? She already loved this unborn child desperately, but would that be enough to provide an emotionally healthy environment?

The baby began kicking vigorously, something that seemed to occur every night at ten or eleven. Libby smiled and laid a hand on her stomach. It seemed to her that the baby was tap-dancing. "It won't be long now, Cupcake," she whispered, and changed position, ignoring the dog's disgruntled sigh. The baby finally quieted down. Libby turned a page in her book, but found herself thinking about Zac instead of what she was reading.

She changed position again, trying to concentrate. But instead, her breast tingled and she remembered Zac's touch. He'd cradled her breast so gently and . . . *hiccup*. Her abdomen jerked. The baby had hiccups. Libby sighed and got out of bed. The baby was not going to let her sleep. Apparently neither was Zac.

This could have been a perfect date, Zac thought as he pulled up in front of Libby's house. After all, he was about to spend an afternoon with an attractive, intelligent woman with a flawless complexion and midnight eyes. The only fly in the ointment was the fact that she was pregnant. That was a pretty big fly. He didn't want kids. He didn't like kids. And they hated him.

All things considered, he'd better make sure this was nothing more than a pleasant, casual afternoon. That decision was sorely tested, however, the moment Libby opened the door. Her hair swung in a sleek, shiny curtain to her waist. It was beautiful hair. Sexy hair. Hair meant to fall around a man when they made love.

She wore a silky blue dress that almost matched the lighter sparkles in her blue eyes. The short, flirty dress showed off her long, slim legs and clung to perfectly shaped breasts—as well as a perfectly rounded abdomen.

His gaze fastened on that abdomen for a moment, then lowered to her feet, encased in sturdy low-heeled walking shoes. He wondered if she ever wore sexy high heels. "You look . . . very nice." Watch it, Webster, he warned himself. He'd been about to tell her she looked gorgeous.

Trouble. Pure trouble. She smiled at him—that same warm smile that seemed to curl right around his heart and squeeze. Why did Hannah get him into these things? He should have known she'd try it, though. Not only was she always telling Zac that he needed to settle down with a wife and family, she'd taken an instant liking to Libby. That was a deadly combination.

Not that Zac couldn't understand. He'd taken an instant liking to Libby himself. *Don't kid yourself, buster. It's a little more complicated than instant liking. More like instant lust.* Somehow, it felt almost sacrilegious to be lusting after a pregnant Madonna. "Don't forget your purse."

TWO

"I'm really looking forward to seeing that exhibit," Libby confided as she got in his car.

"You must be a big fan of pre-Columbian art."

"That's only part of it. The really exciting part is the orchid exhibit that's going on at the same time." Her eyes sparkled with enthusiasm.

"You didn't mention the orchid exhibit last night."

"I thought everybody knew about it."

"Not everybody." Zac's grip tightened on the steering wheel. He didn't care much for plants, any kind of plants. They took up time and space and dropped leaves all over the carpet. The green was nice to look at, he supposed, but that's what fake plants were for. "Orchids. Aren't they parasites, or something?"

"No, they're epiphytes, meaning they live up

on trees, but they don't send roots down into the tree and live off it like a real parasite does."

"I guess they're not carnivorous either."

"Carnivorous?" Libby looked at Zac with amusement. "Where do you get these ideas from?"

"I read an H. G. Wells story once about a giant orchid that overcame its victims with a sweet scent and then sent out its roots to suck their blood."

Libby's eyes lit up. "You read H. G. Wells? So do I! He's always been one of my favorites. I even named my dog after him."

"You named your dog H.G.?"

"No," she giggled. "Wells. H. G. Wells fired a lot of fantasies when I was young."

Me too, Zac thought glumly. One more thing in common. "I know. He did the same for me." He wished Libby would stop looking at him with those glimmering midnight eyes.

"Which of his stories did you like the best?"

"*The Time Machine*. I used to spend hours pretending I'd traveled to different times and places. Maybe it had something to do with being the youngest of three kids and wanting to get away from persecution. How about you?"

"I loved *The Invisible Man*. With Dad being a minister, everything I did always came under such close scrutiny that I wanted to be invisible. That way, I could pass notes and giggle in school like all the other kids, wear my skirts as short and my hair as shaggy."

"Must've been pretty rough on you being a preacher's kid."

"Not really. Dad is pretty open and I doubt he'd have batted an eye had I hiked up my skirt a few inches or brought home a note from the teacher about talking too much. It was everyone else back home that had the expectations."

"Where's home?"

"Home is a small town in Maine, south of Portland."

"How did you wind up in Pennsylvania?"

"I went to college here and stayed when I met Bobby. After he left, I thought about going home, but I have friends here and a job I really love."

"Do you hear from your ex-husband at all?"

She paused for a moment as if she didn't want to answer. "I got a letter from Nassau a few weeks ago telling me that he and his current bimbo were getting married. I don't know where he is now, though."

"Current bimbo," Zac repeated. "Do you resent her?" Was Libby secretly jealous of her because she was still in love with the low-down, no-good son of a— He called an abrupt halt to his wayward thoughts. It shouldn't matter to him whether she was in love with ten men or not.

"Resent her? Hell, no! If anything, I feel sorry for her now that she's got Bobby on her hands."

"Does he know about the baby?"

Libby explained what had happened, then added, "That's why I really have a lot of respect for you."

"Me?" Zac parked the car in front of the museum and turned to Libby. "Why me?"

"Because you're standing by Hannah and staying so involved in the baby's birth, even though you're—you're not—um—living together."

Zac looked confused. "We've never lived together. I thought you realized—she's my sister-in-law. My brother Ben's wife." He eyed her strangely. "All this time you thought we were married?"

She ignored his question. "I have even more respect for you, then, for standing by her," she said softly. "So where's Ben?"

"He's not where he should be," Zac said shortly. "We'd better go in."

Through the rest of the afternoon Zac seemed to be making a concerted effort to keep things carefully impersonal. Libby grew tired of trading inanities like "I love the primitive earthiness of this one" or "That one certainly is interesting." It was as if he'd decided to keep their relationship from going any farther.

But his composure slipped a little when they came to a collection of statues of short, stout females with big breasts and very round abdomens. Libby watched as Zac reached out and rubbed the tips of his fingers across the protruding stomach of one of the figurines. When he turned a brooding gaze on her, she realized that it bothered him that she was pregnant. It bothered him a great deal.

"I guess she's supposed to be a fertility goddess," she said lamely.

"I guess."

"I expect you've seen enough pregnant women the last couple of weeks to last you a good while."

Zac shrugged and gave a noncommittal smile, but he watched her pensively the rest of the afternoon. The most appealing and interesting woman he'd come across in years and she was having a baby. Zac wondered briefly what kind of relationship they might have had had they both been unencumbered.

But she did have a baby on the way, and he had his company. In a way, his computer programming business was every bit as much a baby as the real thing. It kept him up at night; it took all of his time and most of his energy. He certainly didn't have much left to devote to a relationship, though Libby made him wish otherwise.

She had an old-fashioned charm that seemed an inherent part of her, and she had that intriguing surface serenity. But he'd seen flashes of fire in her eyes that hinted at deep-seated passions inside.

One look at her stomach was all it took to remind him that she wasn't for him. Yet something about Libby made Zac begin to think of pregnancy as something sensual. She looked . . . ripe. Like a peach, soft and sweet.

It was a darned shame, he told himself later as he sat on his white leather sofa and stared at his tropical fish. A darned shame.

Libby and Deb waved to Hannah across the room of pregnant women, then went over to sit by her.

"Where's Zac?" Libby asked casually as she sneaked a glance around the room.

"He's in the back corner, hogging the coffee-pot."

Libby wasn't surprised. Since their one and only date two weeks earlier, he'd made every effort to avoid her. It was obvious even to her—and she'd often been told that when it came to subtleties, she was as dense as a London fog.

She tried not to be hurt that he apparently wasn't attracted to her. Not that she looked much like a femme fatale just then. Still, she liked Zac enormously—especially after finding out he was coaching his sister-in-law in his brother's absence. And he was coaching her despite the fact that, according to Hannah, he'd rather be having a root canal. It added to his appeal that he was nice in addition to being sexy as hell.

"What happened when you saw the doctor yesterday?" Hannah was asking.

"He said it will probably be another couple of weeks, even though I'm due next week. I haven't started dilating or anything. How about you?"

"Right on schedule. He said it could be any time now. Zac would prefer to wait as long as possible. He doesn't think he's ready for this yet."

"Ready for what?" Zac asked as he neared the women, his gaze going immediately to Libby. She looked better every time he saw her, even with the circles beneath her eyes. His own eyes narrowed in concern. Obviously she wasn't sleeping well. Although, according to the Lamaze instructor, that wasn't unusual. He wondered if anyone was looking after Libby—making sure she propped her feet up every afternoon, making sure she ate properly.

"Hannah says you're not ready for the baby."

She cocked her head toward Hannah, who, along with Deb, had turned to join a group of classmates in conversation.

"I'm as ready as I'll ever be," he muttered. "How about you? I suppose you're thrilled at the prospect of going through labor."

Libby gave a serene smile. "I'm not worried about it."

"Why not?" Zac sank to the floor beside her, arranging his long legs out in front of him. He glanced at his watch. Class wasn't due to start for another few minutes yet.

"Well, the stress management and guided imagery I've learned here certainly helps, but it's more the realization that this is all a normal part of being a woman. And that there's a reason for labor. I think that we appreciate only what we've had to sweat for. Maybe labor is a physical way of"— she paused to search for the right words— "of preparing us emotionally for the changes that occur once the baby comes."

Her thoughts seemed to turn inward then, concentrating on the life growing inside her. Zac watched, captivated by the soft, unfocused look in her midnight eyes. One slim, graceful hand absently rubbed the curve of her stomach, as if caressing the baby within.

Without thinking, he reached over and covered her hand with his. She looked up, and their gazes held as she slid her hand from beneath his and placed it on top, pressing his palm into her abdomen. The baby moved then, and Zac found himself grinning.

"That's a future ball player," he said softly.

"Or ballet dancer."

"Do you want a girl?"

"It doesn't matter." Libby shook her head, causing long, shimmering tendrils of hair to fall about her face.

Zac lifted his hand from her stomach and brushed back her hair, his fingers lingering on the silky strands, then finding the curved shell of her ear peeking through. He traced its shape with his finger. Libby's eyes widened and he dropped his hand, forcibly wrapping his fingers around his cup of decaf. He was relieved when class began.

But he had trouble listening to the instructor, his thoughts were so preoccupied with Libby. He had plans, he reminded himself, and there was no room in them for a relationship, much less a wife and family. At least not for the next few years. And yet, try as he might to avoid it, he couldn't deny that he wanted Libby. It was the baby he didn't want. For his own peace of mind he had to stay as far away from her as possible.

Hannah wasn't inclined to cooperate, however. The minute she got into Zac's car after class, she turned to him with a bright smile. "I told Libby we'd give her a ride next week. We both want to try out that new Italian restaurant near the mall, and I figured we could go there and eat before class.

"Hannah—"

"And this might be my last chance to get out before the baby."

"Hannah."

"Yes, Zac?" She smiled at him.

Zac sighed. "What time do we pick up Libby?"

"What did your doctor say this week?" Hannah asked the minute Libby got into the car.

Libby gave a patient sigh. "He still says it will be a couple of weeks."

"Isn't that what he said last week?"

"Go figure. It's just as well, since Deb had to go out of town on an emergency. Her brother's having surgery, and she isn't due back till day after tomorrow." She turned to Zac and smiled self-consciously. "Hi."

He felt the same peculiar tightening around his heart he always felt. He was beginning to like it. Dammit. He forced an answering smile. "Hi, yourself."

"Are we still going to Spaghetti Plus for dinner?"

"If that's all right with you."

"Sounds great." Libby sighed with delight. "I just love Italian food."

"Cravings?"

"No, I just like Italian food, that's all."

So did he. Drat, another thing in common. He had no idea just how much in common it was until she placed her order. The antipasto appetizer followed by shrimp scampi and grilled zucchini with basil was exactly what Zac would have ordered. Out of sheer orneriness he ordered baked ziti and broiled tomatoes.

They chatted casually during dinner, though Libby grew quieter toward the end of the meal. "Are you going to eat the rest of those shrimp?" Zac asked, covetously eyeing the pink morsels curled on their bed of pasta.

Libby winced and rubbed her lower back. "No. I don't seem to be as hungry as I thought. Do you want them?"

"If you're sure you don't."

"I'm sure. I have a catch in my back that's driving me crazy. Maybe that's affected my appetite."

"Zac could rub it for you if you like," Hannah offered.

It did sound good, Libby thought wistfully—
the idea of his large, strong hands on her body.
She glanced at him and saw the look on his face. It
wasn't a look of distaste more a look of What?
Here in the restaurant?

"No, it's all right," she murmured. "I'm sure
it'll get better once I get up and move around a
little."

Hannah looked doubtful. "Well, if you're
sure . . ."

Libby forced a smile, not wanting to worry
them. She wasn't sure at all; her lower back had
ached off and on all day, but it seemed worse now.
"I'm fine. I guess it's about time for us to get to
class, isn't it?"

She wholeheartedly threw herself into Lamaze
class. When the visualization and breathing exer-
cises helped, she began to suspect she was in early
labor. The pains hadn't been very regular, but had
been increasing in intensity. She didn't say anything to Zac or Hannah, wanting to talk to her
doctor first. The minute she arrived home from
class, she called Dr. Morgan.

"Back labor," he chuckled. "Throws a lot of
people off. They're expecting pains in front. How
frequently have they been coming?"

"I don't mean to sound stupid, but I don't

know. They haven't been regular at all, but they are getting stronger."

"Why don't you come on over to the hospital and let me check it out? Don't break your neck getting here, though; first babies usually take their sweet time. So relax."

Relax? How in the world am I supposed to relax? I'm in labor! She laid the receiver back in the cradle and stared at the far wall. She'd waited, planned for, and prayed about this day coming, and now that it was here, she wasn't ready. She wasn't at all ready. The phone rang and Libby reached a trembling hand out to it. It was Hannah.

"Libby, you seemed so quiet tonight that I've been worried about you. Are you sure you feel okay?"

Libby took a deep breath and willed her heart to quit its frantic pounding in her ears. "Actually, Hannah, I just talked to my doctor, and he seems to think I'm in labor."

"In labor?" she squealed. "I'm going to send Zac over."

She hung up before Libby could say a word. When the phone rang two minutes later, she knew it had to be Zac.

"Are you in labor?" he barked into the phone.

"I think so."

"I'll be right over." The phone went dead, and

Libby shook her head and hung up the receiver. God, she was scared. And nervous. And excited. She wanted to laugh, she wanted to cry, she wanted to go to sleep and wake up when it was all over.

She did none of those things. She didn't have the luxury of time. She figured it was about twenty minutes from Zac's house to hers. Maybe she'd have time for a shower. She braided her hair to keep it out of the way, made a couple of phone calls, and brought her suitcase downstairs.

She was getting ready to go back upstairs and duck in the shower when Zac showed up. She glanced at the mantel clock. Ten minutes. He hustled her straight out to the car and she got in, surprised there wasn't a speeding citation lying on the seat.

He started the car, then turned to her. "Do you have everything?" He glanced down at a notebook in his hand. "Do you have lollipops, lip moisturizer, socks, uh, cassette player, focal point, uh, your suitcase, the baby's things? Do you need to call anyone else? Are you preregistered at the hospital?"

She smiled, touched by his nervous concern. Strange, she didn't feel nervous at all now. She felt as if she could handle anything as long as Zac was with her. "Yes, no, and yes."

"Huh?"

"Yes, I have everything, including my suitcase and the baby's things. No, I don't need to call anyone—I've already done that. Yes, I'm preregistered."

"Have you already called Deb?"

"I left a message at her hotel in Boston, but I don't know if she'll get here in time." Her voice sounded so calm, she thought. No one would ever know how nervous she was—not unless they saw her hands twisted together in her lap.

"You mean you're in labor and Deb's not here? What are you going to do about a coach?"

Libby bit her lip. Having to go through something as intimate as labor with a total stranger was the last thing she wanted to do. This was an experience to share with someone special. The loneliness that had been her constant companion for the past months swept over her again. "I don't know," she finally said hesitantly. "Maybe one of the nurses can help."

"You mean you're in labor and you don't have a coach at all?" Zac's voice got louder with each word.

Didn't he think she'd already realized that? "Well, I can't see where I have much of a choice," Libby retorted sardonically. "I could always forbid the baby to come until Deb can get here, but somehow I don't think he or she is going to listen. Hey, you ran a red light back there."

"Do you want to drive?" Zac grated out the words.

"If my car were repaired, I would have done exactly that—and without running any lights either."

"Nothing's wrong with the way I drive. I always drive like this."

"It's a wonder your car hasn't more dents than it—" She broke off abruptly.

"Another one?"

"Yes," she said through gritted teeth.

"Are you breathing?"

"Except when I'm talking to you." She took a deep cleansing breath, then turned to Zac. "By the way, would you mind stopping by the drugstore before we get to the hospital?"

"Drugstore! What in the world do you need at the drugstore?"

"I need one of those little car air fresheners in lemon or strawberry."

"What?"

"Weren't you listening when the Lamaze instructor talked about aromatherapy and how these pleasant smells can be used to mask that hospital odor?"

Had he been there? wondered Zac. Yes, he'd

been there all right, immersed in thoughts of her. He pulled into the parking lot of the first drugstore he came to. "I'll run in and get something. You wait here in the car."

Two minutes later he was back. "They don't have strawberry or lemon."

"Could you see if they have vanilla?"

"Vanilla. Gotcha."

Three minutes later he was back with a paper bag. "I found the vanilla. Do you need anything else?"

Libby finished counting her breaths, checked her watch, then answered, "Not a thing."

"How far apart are the contractions?"

"The last two were four minutes apart. This one was eight minutes later."

"You know, if we called Mabel, she'd do it."

"Do what?"

"Coach you through labor."

"I already called her, but I didn't get an answer."

Zac ran his finger around his collar. Suddenly his shirt seemed too tight. "Well, if she doesn't get the message in time, I'm sure there will be a nurse who can help you. That's what you said. Right?"

"Oh, I'm sure," she murmured.

Zac wished she *sounded* sure. He'd just leave

her in the hands of the medical professionals. That's all he'd promised Hannah he'd do. He certainly didn't plan to be Libby's Lamaze coach. He had no intention of being her Lamaze coach. He glanced at Libby and saw her breathing through another contraction. Still, it didn't seem right for her to be going through this alone.

Surely somebody would show up. Maybe Deb would, but just to be sure, he'd try Mabel's number again when they reached the hospital.

The nurse finished hooking up the fetal monitor and turned to leave. "You need to wear this for twenty minutes. This might be a good time to try the positive imagery you learned in Lamaze. You know, they didn't have all these new stress management techniques when I had my twins fifteen years ago."

Zac took the chair next to the bed and stretched his feet out in front of him. "Okay, what's your fantasy?"

"What do you mean, what's my fantasy?" Libby looked up from the fetal heart monitor she'd been watching with interest.

"For the imagery."

"You're going to try imagery?" Libby's eyes widened in mock surprise. "But Hannah said you have absolutely no imagination."

Zac looked affronted. "I have a great imagination. Anyway, I can do this until Deb gets here, or I can get hold of Mabel. You just lay your head back on the bed and listen."

Libby complied, getting comfortable. After all, she had to stay hooked up to the fetal monitor for the next twenty minutes anyway. And she really did want to hear what kind of fantasy Zac would come up with. She had more curiosity about him than was good for her. Besides, listening to him talk made her feel safe, secure. "Okay, I'm ready."

"This is supposed to be your fantasy, so you should come up with an idea."

"Why don't you surprise me?" Libby laid her head back on the pillow and watched his face. He had a nice face, she thought—extra-determined jaw, though. He was probably stubborn and opinionated. He was also strong and dependable.

"Okay. Close your eyes and relax. We're going to the mountains. There's a rustic lodge with a huge stone firepl—"

Libby opened her eyes and made a face. "I don't like cold weather."

Zac rolled his eyes. "How about the beach?"

"I love the beach." She closed her eyes again.

"We're getting on a boat. It's a fifty-foot cabin cruiser and—"

"I don't like boats."

"But you said you like the beach."

Libby opened one eye and peered at him. "I do like the beach. The beach, Zac, that means warm sand and waves and all that."

"But that's boring."

Libby opened her other eye and pursed her lips. "Whose fantasy is this supposed to be anyway?"

Zac sighed. "Fine. You're walking on a warm, sandy beach. Feel the warmth travel from your feet to your legs, to your thighs, through your whole body, all the way to your fingertips. There's a cool breeze off the ocean, and you can feel the mist on your face." He glanced at the monitor and noticed a contraction beginning.

"Take a deep breath of that breeze. Continue to take slow deep breaths . . . slow deep breaths . . ." Zac kept one eye on the monitor. "Okay, now a deep cleansing breath. That's good."

"They're getting stronger," Libby murmured.

"They're supposed to. Now, back to the beach." He continued to describe the beach scene until the nurse came in to unhook Libby from the monitor.

Libby smiled gratefully. "I can get up and move around now, right?"

"Right. Walking around will speed up labor a bit. And it will help your back labor too."

Libby sat on the edge of the bed and looked at Zac. "Um, I guess you'll be leaving now," she said, and looked down at her entwined fingers. *Please, please don't go*, she begged silently.

Zac looked at her for several moments. "I . . . well, I'll stay until we get someone else, okay? I'm sure Deb will be here or we'll get in touch with Mabel soon."

Zac walked Libby up and down the hospital corridor for what seemed like hours to her. Every time she had a contraction, she stopped, grabbed hold of Zac, and breathed. In between her contractions she thought over and over of how strong Zac was, how caring, how supportive.

After one particularly bad contraction she looked down, vaguely surprised at the puddle of water on the floor. "Uh-oh."

"What do you mean uh-oh?"

"I think my water just broke."

"Uh-oh."

THREE

"My notebook . . . I can't find it." Zac frantically patted his pockets.

Why was he worried about his notebook, she wondered, when she was soaking wet? Libby grimaced as her wet gown clung to her legs, but said matter-of-factly, "I think I should go back to my room and you should probably get a nurse and tell her what happened so they can mop the floor."

Zac turned, hooked his arm around her, and began walking her back to the room. "You amaze me."

"Why?"

"Because you're so calm and in control. I really admire that. But you're in labor, for Pete's sake. A little nervousness is allowed."

He was nervous enough for the both of them, Libby thought, and forced back her own jitters.

"Women have babies every day," she said, pleased at how controlled she sounded. "I don't know why you're getting so rattled. Hannah said you're usually the epitome of cool control."

"I'm not rattled," Zac denied emphatically. "Anyway, I've never been through labor before."

"Neither have I. You're not going to fall apart on Hannah, are you?"

"Of course not. I haven't exactly fallen apart on you either. But her husband should be here for this."

"Where is he?"

"God only knows. He didn't even acknowledge when she sent him a letter telling him she was pregnant. He's always been a rolling stone, but I never thought he was an idiot too."

"Must be hard on her going through this alone."

"You're doing it."

"I have no choice."

"Does your ex-husband—" He broke off when Libby grabbed his arm. He put his hands at her waist and supported her while she lay her forehead on his chest. "Slow, even breaths . . . that's it . . . slow and even . . . it's almost over . . . cleansing breath. Great."

She continued to stand there, leaning on him. It felt so good to be taken care of, however briefly.

As if sensing she needed the closeness, Zac put his arms around her and held her.

"It's all right, baby. You're doing fine," he murmured against the top of her head. "Are you getting tired?"

"A little."

"Not ready to run any marathons, I guess."

She shook her head and curled her fingers into the smooth fabric of his shirt. "I feel like I already have. Do you think I can do it, Zac? Maybe I should just go ahead and have the epidural."

"Is that what you want to do?"

"No. I just want to do what's best for my baby."

"I think what's best for you is best for the baby. Go for broke, Libby." He laid his cheek against the top of her head and squeezed her close. "I don't have any doubts at all that you can do it."

"But what will I do if we can't find Mabel or if Deb doesn't show up? Zac, I don't want a stranger to coach me." She knew she was playing on his sympathy but didn't care. She didn't want anyone but Zac with her.

"Don't worry. It'll work out."

"I can't help worrying. Please stay with me, Zac. I know it's a lot to ask, but I don't think I could go through this with a stranger."

Zac sighed, as if giving in to the inevitable. "I'll stay."

Libby leaned her head tiredly against his shoulder and allowed him to help her back to her room. Her contractions became stronger and closer together. Zac rubbed her lower back to help ease the almost constant ache. As labor intensified, Libby withdrew into herself, quiet and preoccupied, trying to stay on top of the contractions. Yet through it all she remained aware of Zac's presence, his encouragements, his patience.

During the contractions he breathed along with her. In between he wiped her forehead with a cool cloth, offered her ice chips, applied lip balm to her dry lips, even put socks on her chilly feet. He seemed to know instinctively when she needed distracting chatter and when she needed quiet.

The contractions were now lasting a minute and a half and were only a minute apart. Zac marveled at her strength, her intensity, her beauty. She still retained that inherent air of serenity, although Zac could tell by the lines of effort etched into her brow and the beads of sweat on her face that it was being strained. And though he hadn't wanted to stay, he was fiercely glad that he was there for her.

"I'm so tired," she suddenly moaned, and grabbed his hand. "I can't do this anymore."

"Yes, you can. It's not going to be long now." He tenderly stroked tendrils of hair back from her face. "Think about the baby, Libby," he urged. "How soft his skin is going to feel, how tiny his little hands and feet will be. How right it's going to feel to hold him. You can do it, baby, I know you can. It's just a little bit longer now, and then—"

"Oh, God, it's another one. I can't do it anymore. I can't."

Zac grabbed her hands and looked straight into her eyes, trying to infuse her with his strength. "Yes, you can. Breathe with me, baby. Breathe with me."

It was only a few minutes later when Libby suddenly caught her breath. "Zac? Something's different. There's a lot of pressure and I . . . oh. I need to push."

"You can't!" Zac exclaimed, his heart pounding. This was it. He grabbed the signal and pushed the nurse-call button. "Don't do anything until the nurse gets here." He frantically searched through his head for what they were supposed to do in this situation.

"What are we supposed to do now? I know you're not supposed to push until the nurse gets here," he muttered. "My mind seems to have gone blank." *Where the hell is my notebook?* He tugged it out of his back pocket and flipped a few pages. *Pant. That's it.* "You're supposed to pant."

"Okay, Libby. Blow out. Short little puffs . . . come on, you can do it. Lean your head back more . . . come on. Little puffs . . . that's it . . . that's it."

The nurse came in and examined Libby. "Well, I think we're about ready to push. Let's put the head of the bed up a little higher. With the next contraction, lean forward and grab your knee. Let your coach grab the other. Then take a deep breath, let it out, take another, and hold it."

Another contraction and she pushed as Zac encouraged her. The nurse examined her again after a few minutes. "Whoa! You're quite an efficient pusher. I need to call the doctor in. Don't push until he gets here."

"What do you mean, don't push?" Libby cast a panicked glance at Zac. "I don't think I can stop pushing. Oh, here comes another one. Zac—"

"It's okay, baby. Lean your head back and blow out. Short puffs . . . short puffs. You can do it. . . . Now, take a deep cleansing breath. . . . See? That wasn't so bad."

Libby cast him a venomous look. "And just how many babies have you had recently? What do you know about it?"

"I know that you're getting crotchety in your old age."

"Who's old? I am a mere babe in arms? . . . Oh, God, here it comes. I've got to push, Zac."

"No. Now blow out. Come on. Blow out. Dammit, stop pushing, Libby! Stop pushing! Libby? . . . Libby!"

"Zac! What happened? Is everything all right? How's Libby?" Deb came running over to where Zac sat in the lounge, staring out the window into the early morning sun.

He turned a bemused gaze on her. "She had the baby, Deb."

"What's wrong with the baby? Is it all right?"

He went on as if he hadn't heard. "The doctor wasn't even in the room. The nurse wasn't there. It was just me and her and then out pops this little baby, right into my hands." Zac looked up at Deb. "It's a girl. A beautiful, bald-headed little girl. She looked at me with these big dark blue eyes and screamed bloody murder."

"Is Libby all right?"

"She's fine. She was amazing, really. I don't think I've ever met a woman as strong and determined as she is. She kept her cool the whole time." He shook his head. "She's amazing," he repeated.

"What's she doing now?"

"I think she's asleep."

"How about you? Are you okay? You look a little frazzled to me."

"Oh, no. I'm fine. I'm just fine." He forced a smile. "I'm tired, though. I didn't sleep at all, so I think I'll go home."

"You aren't going to wait for Libby to wake up?"

Zac sighed. "I don't think so. She'll be too interested in the baby. She won't even notice I'm gone."

"She'll notice," murmured Deb, but she said it to the back of Zac's rumpled shirt as he disappeared down the hall.

"Where's Zac?" Libby smiled at Deb, then yawned.

"He was tired, so he went home."

"Oh." Libby tried to keep the disappointment out of her voice. "Have you seen little Cupcake yet?"

"I peeked in the nursery on the way in here. She's a real doll."

"Isn't she? Zac was so wonderful. He was so patient, and he never left me for a minute. He was right there the whole time. He's a terrific coach. A terrific man."

Deb eyed her curiously. "Sounds like it."

"He even rubbed my back—I had horrible back labor. And he walked with me up and down the halls forever, it seemed. I was about ready to chuck it in at one point, but he wouldn't let me. He took my hands and breathed right along with me. Did I tell you he rubbed my back for me?"

"I think you did," Deb murmured.

"He delivered my baby. Did you know that? The doctor took too long to get there, and she just wouldn't wait to be born. So Zac delivered her." Her face softened. "He cried when he held her, Deb. He tried to hide it, but I saw him."

"Then what happened?"

"Then the doctor got there, cut the cord, and laid her on my chest. She made all these little baby noises and looked at me for the longest time without blinking. I could swear she really saw me, really knew who I was."

Deb smiled and shook her head. "You know, Libby, I've known you since college, and I don't think I've ever seen you this wound up before. Zac said even labor didn't rattle you."

"It didn't, but it's because Zac wouldn't let me get rattled. Besides, I knew what to expect, and it really wasn't all that bad. I just kept focusing on Zac and Cupcake."

"Speaking of the baby, you're not planning on enrolling her in kindergarten as Cupcake, are you?"

"No. I'm going to name her Victoria, after my grandmother."

"How about a middle name?"

"I'm not sure yet."

"I think Hannah said Zac's middle name is Dane," Deb said slyly.

Libby's face lit up. "Dane. Victoria Dane Austen. That does have a nice ring to it, doesn't it?"

For the first time in ten years Zac took a day off.

"Not coming in? Not coming in?" his secretary repeated. "Are you in the hospital or something?"

"No, I'm fine. I'm just taking the day off. It's allowed, you know. I'm the boss."

"Well, yes, but—"

"I'll be in tomorrow," he said in dismissal, and hung up the phone. He sat on the sofa and watched his tropical fish swim around. He ought to go to bed, he mused. After all, he hadn't slept at all the night before. Somehow, though, he didn't think he'd sleep for the next week.

All he could see was the look on Libby's face when they laid the baby on her chest. Even covered in perspiration, with tangled hair long since escaped from her braid, and mascara smudges beneath her eyes, she'd been the most beautiful woman he'd ever seen.

He remembered how she had fumbled with the top of her gown when she prepared to nurse the baby for the first time. Her cheeks had pinkened in embarrassment at the room full of people, but her gaze had locked with Zac's as she guided the baby's seeking mouth to the waiting nipple. Her eyes had widened in awe and her smile had glowed. She looked as if she'd been handed a miracle. Maybe she had. Zac had felt unaccustomed tears sting his eyes and couldn't help but stand there and watch.

He yawned and leaned his head back on the sofa, remembering the way the baby had felt in his arms. Maybe it was a miracle. He yawned again and closed his eyes.

FOUR

"Why do I have to go to this reunion thing?" Zac asked the moment Hannah opened the door.

"Because you were my Lamaze coach." She added, "And Libby's."

"Not by choice," he muttered, already fastening the infant seat in the front of his car. He ignored the "and Libby" part just as he'd tried to ignore all thoughts of her the past six weeks. He'd done a good job of it too. During the day, at least.

At night, however, the minute he fell asleep she came waltzing uninvited into his head with her swath of satiny hair, her sinful legs, lush breasts, and tempting mouth. But every time he reached out for her, all he got was a baby that stared at him with unblinking blue eyes, then wailed.

"Look, I'll come back and pick you and Nicky up in a couple of hours, okay?"

"Nothing doing, sugar. You're going in."

"Wait," he said as Hannah opened the car door and got out. "The babies will probably all scream when they see me. You know kids don't like me."

"That's a bunch of nonsense. I don't know why you keep insisting kids don't like you. If they cry, it's because they sense you're scared to death of them."

"With good reason," Zac muttered.

"Don't be silly," Hannah again admonished him as she unfastened the baby from the seat and hoisted him into her arms. "It'll be interesting to see what everyone else had, don't you think?"

Zac sighed, rubbed the back of his neck, and followed Hannah to the door of Mabel's house. Inside, the first thing he did was look for Libby. When he didn't see her, he wasn't sure if he was happy or sorry.

"Here's the coach of the year." Mabel came over. "You should win an award for service above and beyond the call of coaching." She hoisted the baby she was holding higher up on her shoulder and turned her attention to Hannah and Nicky.

Libby saw Zac the minute he walked in the door. She stood in the far corner, next to a large ficus tree, and peered through the foliage. She wasn't trying to hide from Zac, she told herself. She wasn't. She was just trying to give him what he wanted—and what he wanted apparently was as little contact with her as possible.

That had been made abundantly clear in the weeks since Victoria's birth. He'd sent two dozen miniature pink roses to the hospital the day after she delivered, with a terse congratulatory note. And that was the last she'd seen of him.

She thought she'd seen him sitting in his red sports car across the street from her house that same afternoon Deb brought her home from the hospital. But by the time she put the baby down in her new cradle and went back to the front door, the car was gone.

He hadn't called, not even when she'd left a message with his secretary. He did send a teddy bear with a pink satin bow around its neck for the baby's one week birthday. At least Libby assumed it was from Zac, since there was no card with it and all her other friends denied sending it.

Libby was surprised Hannah had persuaded Zac to come to the Lamaze class reunion. He had the same uncomfortable expression on his face that he'd had the first time she'd seen him— definitely a fight-or-flee look. She couldn't stand behind the plant all night, she thought, and ran her hands down the front of her rose-pink sundress. Pasting a bright smile on her face, she stepped into plain view.

Zac saw her immediately. She couldn't tell how he felt about seeing her—his face was expressionless. But he did make his way over to her.

"How are you?"

"I'm just fine," she murmured politely. "And you?"

"Oh, fine. How's, uh, the baby?"

"Victoria's beautiful."

"Yeah. Hannah said you'd named her Victoria."

"Victoria Dane."

Zac looked stunned. "Dane?"

"Hannah didn't tell you?"

"No, I didn't," Hannah said, coming up behind Zac. "I thought you should be the one to tell him he has an almost namesake."

"Why?" Zac asked, paying no attention to Hannah.

"I owed you," Libby murmured. "And you never gave me a chance to thank you."

Zac could feel his cheeks grow warm at her words. "I—I just did what—what any other man would have done in the same circumstances." Damn! What was there about this woman that made him feel as tongue-tied as a teenager on his first date?

"No, I don't think so. What you did only a very special man could have done. I don't know how I can ever thank you. I never would have made it through labor without you there."

Zac felt like running his finger around his collar as he stared into her beautiful blue eyes. For a brief moment he found himself wondering if her eyes got lighter when she made love—as light as the silver-blue sparkles in them—or if they darkened to almost black. Then he shook the thought away, shoved his hands into his pockets, and shrugged. "No thanks needed."

"Yes, there are. You were so supportive, so patient. You seemed to know exactly what I needed at any given moment."

"A regular paragon of virtue, right?" he scoffed lightly.

She smiled, that same heart-hugging smile, and said, "Would you believe I'm nominating you for sainthood next week?" She eyed him curiously. "You don't like to be complimented, do you?"

"Hey, I like it as well as the next guy, it's just that—" He broke off, not sure exactly what it was he wanted to say. He *did* like compliments, but somehow, coming from her, they made him uncomfortable. As far as compliments went, though, there were plenty he could think of about her and that rose-pink dress she wore.

The last time he'd seen her, she'd been covered with perspiration, with lines of exhaustion etched into her face. Now, however, she took his breath away. There were some things that were the same. Her hair still swung in a shiny, dark drape down her back, and her smooth, creamy skin still glowed. The mile-long legs hadn't changed either, or, if they had, had only gotten better—longer, silkier, more golden.

He followed those legs down to her feet and froze, feeling suddenly light-headed. Her feet were showcased to perfection in strappy white sandals—dainty, small-boned feet with shell-pink toenails. He could imagine her lying next to him in bed, running them up and down his leg. *I'm losing my mind. I've never had a foot fetish before*, he thought, his gaze lingering on her toes. With a concerted effort he turned his attention elsewhere, and things got even worse.

Her swollen abdomen was gone, replaced by a flat stomach and the soft indentation of a waist that flared into gently rounded hips. His gaze followed the curve of those hips back to the waist, then up farther to the lush breasts that strained against the halter top of the sundress.

He then followed the strap of that sundress as

it disappeared around the back of her neck and reappeared on the other side to fasten at the top with one shiny gold button. His eyes lingered on that offensive button. One day, he decided, he was going to rip that button right off. With his teeth.

He felt his trousers become distinctly less comfortable and decided it might be prudent to get his mind onto a safer subject. "Ah, you said the baby's okay."

"She's fine. She's gaining weight and making little noises. All the things six-week-old babies should do. Mabel has her. Do you want to hold her?"

"Ah, no," Zac said quickly. "I, uh, think I may be coming down with a cold."

"I see." She saw all right. She saw that Zac was positively terrified at the idea of holding a baby. Was that why he'd been so scarce the past few weeks? Did he have a phobia about babies, or something? She decided to test her theory. "Gee, you don't sound at all hoarse." She touched her hand to his forehead. "And you're not the least bit feverish. Let me get Cupcake. You won't believe how much she's grown."

Zac cleared his throat and backed up a step. "I wouldn't feel right about exposing her. Just in case, you know."

"Well, if you're sure . . ." Libby let the words trail off, filled with tender amusement by the stark look of relief that flitted across his face. He was too tall, too powerful, too masculine to be reduced to terror at the very mention of a baby. She wished she could erase the fear.

Why didn't he realize that the very gentleness of his large hands called for a baby to caress, that the breadth of his shoulders was made to cradle a baby's head—or a woman's. A surge of longing shot through her. She wanted his shoulder to cradle *her* baby's head—and her own. Libby continued to stare at Zac, a dreamy look on her face.

Zac began to fidget. "You, uh, you said you're doing fine, right?"

"Perfect," she murmured, still gazing at him with a mixture of hope, speculation, and intriguing sexual awareness in her face. He didn't like the way she was looking at him. Or maybe he did. Too much.

She was staring at him with those killer blue-velvet eyes, and her lips were curved in the barest hint of a smile. It was a look guaranteed to knock a man off his feet—or at least knock every last vestige of good sense right out of his head. And since he was still standing, he could only assume that his good sense had been the one to go.

This was proved when he found himself agreeing to have dinner at her house. He couldn't figure out why he'd done it. He didn't need to get mixed up with a woman who came complete with ready-made family. She was probably looking for daddy material, and he wasn't it. So why didn't he simply tell her that he couldn't make it?

Was it because he fantasized about wrapping himself in that hair? Was it because of her fathomless eyes, or was it the smile that took his breath away every time he saw it? Was it because of her strength, her purpose, her serenity? Was it her dry humor or her brains? Maybe it was all of those, he acknowledged honestly. Or—his gaze lit on her feet—maybe it was those tempting little toes peeking out from those sexy sandals.

Libby wiggled her toes as if aware he was staring at her feet, so he forced himself to look up, only to see Deb bearing down on the two of them, baby in tow. Now he did run his finger around his suddenly too-tight collar.

He turned to Libby. "I think I'll get some coffee. Do you want—" He broke off suddenly as Deb thrust the infant into his arms. His hands automatically clutched the baby to him.

"Hasn't she grown?" Deb enthused.

Zac managed a weak smile and surveyed the baby. She had changed since he'd last seen her. She had one tiny dark curl on her otherwise bald head and had the same blue eyes as her mother. She was dressed in green terry and smelled soft and sweet, like baby powder. "That she has."

At the sound of his deep voice, Victoria started and her tiny bottom lip began to quiver. She restlessly kicked her arms and legs and made a little mewling sound in protest. That was all it took. Zac immediately handed the baby to Libby.

"I really need my evening coffee," he said in desperation. "I get mean without caffeine." Actually, caffeine after supper kept him awake, but he'd rather pace the floor until the wee hours than hold a tiny, screaming person in his arms. Not only was it murder on his eardrums, but it was hell on his ego.

Libby calmly cradled her now-cooing daughter in her arms. "I'll go with you. I could use something cool to drink."

"I'll bring you something," Zac offered hastily—anything to get away from the crush of babies that seemed to be coming at him. "What would you like? Coffee? Soft drink? Tea?"

"Juice or a soft drink, either one would be fine. Nothing with caffeine in it, though. It keeps Cupcake up at night."

Now, why'd she have to go and remind him that she was nursing? That was one image he'd tried long and hard to erase from his mind. He thought of her again, the way she'd looked in the hospital when she'd nursed the baby for the first time—the self-conscious blush that almost matched her rosy nipples, the look of surprise, then wonder, as the baby hungrily suckled. God, he really needed that coffee, he thought, and made a determined beeline to the refreshment table.

Libby watched him as he made his way to the far corner of the room. *At least he'd agreed to come to dinner. That's something, I guess.* She then turned her attention to the small daughter nestled contentedly in her arms. "Why'd you have to act up that way, Sweetcakes? He thinks you don't like him."

Victoria just stared up at her mother's face with solemn blue eyes and gurgled.

Libby pressed a soft kiss on the baby's forehead. "Just don't do it anymore, okay? He's really a nice man. A very nice man. He's intelligent and funny and sexy as all get-out—not that you need to worry about sexy just yet."

Hannah waved at Libby and came over, Nicky asleep on her shoulder. "I see you and Zac have been talking."

Libby gave a rueful smile and brushed back an errant strand of hair. "I don't mean to quote clichés, Hannah, but you know that one about a long-tailed cat in a room full of rocking chairs? I get the impression that describes your brother-in-law in a room full of babies."

Hannah nodded. "You've noticed, huh? For some reason, he keeps saying that babies hate him."

"Why does he think that?"

"I'm not saying he really believes that. Part of me is inclined to believe he uses it as an excuse. Personally, I think he thinks kids won't fit into his life. Although, Ben said that when Zac was seventeen or eighteen, he got stuck baby-sitting one of his young cousins who had colic. Ben said that the baby howled all weekend long. And then, there was Pamela's daughter."

"Who's Pamela?"

"His ex-fiancée."

He'd been engaged. Libby wondered if he was still nursing a broken heart. Maybe that's why babies made him uncomfortable—they reminded him of what he'd lost. "How long ago was he engaged?" She tried to sound casual.

"Last year."

"What about the daughter?"

"She was four years worth of spoiled rotten. I think she didn't like the idea of sharing her mommy with anybody. Every time she saw Zac she began screaming her head off. Up until that time Zac figured it was just babies who hated him.

After Pamela, he began to believe it was kids in general."

"Did, ah, did he take the breakup hard?" Libby hoped her interest in Zac wasn't too obvious.

"Not at all. I don't think it was his heart that was damaged. It was his pride. He hadn't gotten engaged because he'd fallen in love; it was more that he felt it was time he got married. At least that's my theory and Ben thought the same thing."

That was the second time Hannah had mentioned her husband's name. "Have you heard from him at all?" she asked gently.

"I just got the signed divorce papers in the mail a few days ago."

"I'm sorry."

"Don't be. Because I'm glad it's over."

"So was I when my divorce became final."

Zac came up behind them in the middle of this conversation and eavesdropped shamelessly.

"How long were you and Bobby married?"

"Four long, lousy years. It was a mistake almost from the beginning."

"Why?"

"Because he had no sense of responsibility. I met him when I was finishing up my master's degree. After six years of school, the last year spent student-teaching, his every-day's-a-holiday attitude seemed to be what I needed at the time. I really thought that once we were married, he'd settle down."

Libby sighed and shifted the baby from one shoulder to the other. "He didn't. He still went out partying almost every night until all hours. And if I didn't want to go, he went anyway. Unfortunately, he was out so late every night, he began oversleeping and he was late to work a lot. He lost seven or eight jobs before finally going to work for his uncle."

Zac cleared his throat and Libby turned around. "Here's your soda." He gave her a cup of ginger ale, then turned to Hannah. "I have to go. I have an early meeting."

Hannah rolled her eyes at Libby and whispered, "Personally, I think he just wants to get out of here—too many babies and all that."

"You're darn right." He'd overheard. He turned to Libby. "I guess you have your car now so you don't need a ride."

She nodded. "At least until the next thing goes wrong with it. Is seven-thirty Friday okay?"

Zac nodded. "See you then." That is, if he didn't manage to talk himself out of it. And he intended to try. Real hard.

FIVE

He'd tried, honestly tried, to break his date. He even got as far as calling Libby. But the minute he'd heard her soft, husky-sweet voice, he'd forgotten what he'd planned to say. So here he was, standing outside Libby's front door, trying to make his legs move. *Come on, you fool, either advance or retreat, but for God's sake, do something.* He knocked.

Libby opened the door almost immediately. He nearly groaned out loud when he saw her. She was wearing some kind of frilly skirt that hit several inches above her knees, and a scoop-neck T-shirt, in sunshine yellow. She looked like a buttercup or daffodil or some other kind of yellow flower, he thought.

The killer, however, was the pair of yellow sandals that showed off her delectable pink-tipped toes. For one brief moment he found himself wondering how they'd taste.

"You, uh, look very nice," he said lamely. "And something smells good."

"The best homemade lasagna on the East Coast. What's that?" She motioned at the bag he held in his left hand.

"A bottle of wine. I didn't know what you were fixing, so I brought a rosé. I hope that's all right."

"It's fine," Libby murmured.

"Where's the baby?" *Please let her be at Grandma's or something*, he asked silently.

"I just put her down to sleep, but I don't think she's nodded off yet." Libby smiled brightly. "Do you want to see her?"

"No! I mean, I'd hate to keep her awake. How long do you think she'll sleep?"

"With any luck at all, until twelve or one." She stifled a sigh at his look of relief. She really liked Zac. A lot. But Victoria had to be her first responsibility now. And if she was going to date, it was going to have to be with Victoria in mind, and that meant a man who really liked children. As much as she liked Zac, maybe seeing him wasn't such a good idea. She wondered about a brief, passionate affair. Maybe that would take care of the incessant itch she felt every time she thought about him. Maybe. But she doubted it.

She took the bottle of wine from Zac and put it on ice to chill. She ran down a list of things to talk about, but her mind seemed to have gone blank. Apparently he couldn't think of anything to talk about either, because the silence dragged on for several minutes. She wished he'd go into the living room and wait. The longer he stood there and watched her, the more nervous she got. It was as if she could feel his gaze on her back.

Zac cleared his throat. "This is a very nice—" A loud, deep "woof" reverberated around the room, and Zac broke off his words and backed up against the kitchen counter. "What in the world?"

A large, silky-haired golden retriever ran into the room, tail wagging so hard that it was hitting itself on either side. The dog paused for all of a tenth of a second before bounding over to Zac and sticking its nose in his crotch.

"He won't hurt you," Libby said quickly.

"I've figured that out." Zac's voice was dry as he fended off the exuberantly affectionate advances of the dog. "I take it this is Wells?"

"Yes. He really seems to like you too."

"Just my luck," Zac muttered and tried to keep the dog from licking his face. "I didn't know they allowed you to keep ponies as house pets."

Libby grabbed Wells's collar and managed to

tug the large animal away. "Okay, sweetie. I think you should go out in the backyard for a little while." She struggled to hold on to the dog with one hand and open the back door with the other.

"Let me." Zac opened the door, and Libby gave Wells a gentle shove.

"Sorry about that," she apologized. "He's very affectionate. He'll be happy out there for a few minutes, anyway. Then he'll have to come back inside."

"Will he run out into the street if you don't bring him in?"

"No, the backyard's fenced. He's really a people dog, and when I put him out, he gets lonely after a few minutes and starts crying."

Zac tried in vain to brush off the golden-white hairs clinging voraciously to his dark trousers.

"So, are there any more like you at home?" Zac finally said, and leaned up against the kitchen counter, crossing his legs at the ankle.

"My sister, Faith, is in her last year of medical school. What about you? I know you have a brother who occasionally persecuted you as well as a brand-new nephew. What about your other brother?"

"Actually, both brothers persecuted me. I was the youngest. There's Ben and Matt. Matt is married and lives in New York. He's got two kids exactly nine months apart—one boy, one girl."

Libby opened the refrigerator and began setting items on the counter. "Do you see your niece and nephew a lot?"

"Ah, no, I don't get up there very often."

"New York isn't exactly half a continent away."

"Yeah, well . . ." He changed the subject. "Can I help you do something?"

"Are you good at chopping veggies?"

"I'm an expert."

Libby handed him a cucumber, a tomato, and a knife. "Prove it." She turned away with the flash of a smile and the flip of her skirt.

Zac turned his attention to the task at hand, then glanced at Libby. "All done." He stopped dead for a moment and made a strangled sound. "What are you doing?"

Libby straightened from where she'd been unbuckling a sandal. "I hope you don't mind. My feet hurt."

His mouth felt suddenly dry. "Go ahead." He watched as she finished unbuckling one sandal and slid it off her dainty foot, then wiggled her toes as if relishing the freedom. That simple act was every bit as erotic as if she'd slipped her blouse over her head. He felt an unmistakable pressure in his groin and turned away before she removed the other shoe, though he strained his ears listening for the telltale sounds.

Lord, what was the matter with him? He'd never had this fixation on feet before. Of course, he acknowledged to himself, he'd never seen feet quite like hers before. He wondered if they were ticklish, and flexed his fingers at the thought of running them lightly down the bottom of her foot. Would Libby laugh or just wriggle her toes?

A sudden disgruntled wail from the other room made Libby straighten. "Oh, dear, Victoria's awake." As she headed to the bedroom, Wells started barking outside the kitchen door. "Would you let him in before he disturbs the neighbors?" she called over her shoulder.

This evening was not turning out at all like Zac had hoped. A little dinner, a little wine, a little romance? Ha! He should have remembered The Plan. Stick with women who know how to play the game and avoid, at all cost, women with fussy babies and barking, shedding dogs.

They ate dinner with Victoria bouncing on her mother's knee and Wells staring down Zac with pleading brown eyes as he leaned against Zac's leg, adding even more hairs to the ones still clinging from earlier. Surprisingly, the conversation went well, or maybe not so surprisingly, since Libby was a charming and intelligent companion. It wasn't her fault she came complete with infant and mutt.

After dinner the baby still wouldn't go back to sleep, so Libby and Zac sat in the living room, drinking decaffeinated coffee while Libby held Victoria. "Maybe if I nursed her . . ." Libby glanced at Zac. "If it's okay with you."

"Sure, go ahead."

Libby angled her body away from Zac, and he could see her fumble with her T-shirt for a moment. Then he heard the unmistakable suckling noises of a contented baby. He forced himself to look away from the bare skin of her back that had been revealed when she tugged up her T-shirt, and found his gaze lingering on her feet again.

He was as aware of her as if she'd been dancing naked in front of him. His skin prickled with her nearness, yet the contented noises of the infant were a powerful deterrent to any more errant thoughts. Their conversation became more stilted and garden-party formal—they even discussed the weather. The silent pauses became longer and more awkward. When Libby got up to put a now-drowsy baby back in her crib, Zac decided to leave before it got even more difficult.

Zac stood when Libby came back into the room after putting the baby down. "It was a terrific dinner. You're right. You do make the best lasagna on the East Coast. Is the baby asleep?"

She smiled. "She's sleeping like, well, like a

baby." Her smile faded. "Do you have to leave?"

"Um, yes. I have an, ah, an early meeting. It's been a nice evening, though."

You've got that same fight-or-flee look again, Mr. Webster. Well, go right ahead and flee. I mean, if a man doesn't like babies, then I can't waste my time on him. Even if he does have nice shoulders, tight buns, and a smile that not only could charm the birds out of the trees, but could likely charm the socks—or whatever—off assorted ladies as well.

From the look on Zac's face, it was obvious he felt the same way Libby did. This was an ill-advised and ill-fated relationship and it was better ended before it began.

"Thanks for the wine," she said. "I'm sure it was terrific."

"Even if you didn't drink any," Zac murmured dryly.

"I'm sorry, I guess I forgot to tell you that Cupcake's a little too young to drink."

Wells groaned in his sleep and rolled over on his back. Zac stared at the lump of fur sprawled across the floor for a moment and decided it was past time to leave. "I'll call you." He knew darn well he wouldn't. There was absolutely nothing in this world that could induce him to get involved with her. With an effort he kept his eyes from straying to her bare toes. Well, almost nothing.

Libby walked with him to the door. "Thank you again, Zac. For everything." She planted a kiss on his cheek.

He wasn't sure how it happened, but suddenly she was in his arms. He moved his mouth over hers, tentatively at first, then with certainty. She tasted like sunshine and raindrops, fluffy clouds and clear skies. Her soft breasts nestled just right against his chest, and her thighs meshed with his.

He pulled back just far enough to see that she stood on dainty pink tiptoe. That was all it took. He'd call her. He had to.

Zac couldn't sleep, and it was all her fault. Dammit! She just had to kiss like an angel, didn't she? Or, then again, maybe it wasn't an angel that she kissed like. It was more like a Lorelei—luring unsuspecting men to their death. But, he found himself thinking, they'd go with smiles on their faces.

He sprawled on his white velour sofa, relishing the quiet of his luxury apartment. No baby noises, no dog noises, nothing but the muted gurgle from his twenty-gallon tropical fish tank.

It was even restful on his eyes—the black and white decor simple and direct. Not at all like the riot of colors that assaulted the senses in her living room. The flowered sofa had pink and green throw pillows piled all over it, while the carpet was some kind of pink, green, and blue design. All of it had been littered liberally with bright dog toys.

Her house abounded with a carnival of aromas—tomato sauce, oregano, the scent from the roses outside the front door, the fresh green smell of the dozens of houseplants elbowing one another for space in front of the windows, and the underlying sweetness of baby powder.

Zac breathed deeply. His own place smelled of . . . nothing. Apparently, his expensive air purifier did a great job. Not even the scent of her hair lingered in his nostrils.

Zac sprinkled a dash of fish food in the aquarium, watching as the black and white angelfish, black mollies, and white tetras swarmed around the particles. Even his fish fit the color scheme of his apartment, he thought—and they didn't shed. He watched the fish for a moment longer, then straightened the line of silk plants on the black marble mantel. Maybe he didn't have a regular jungle of plants in front of his windows, but at least these didn't need to be watered or fertilized.

Finally he picked up the latest business magazine from the coffee table and looked through it. When he found himself reading the same page three times and still not knowing what it said, he tossed the magazine down. He felt restless for some reason he didn't care to define. Maybe a half-hour workout in the gym downstairs would cure it.

Forty-five minutes, a workout, and a shower later, and he was still restless. He flipped through every channel on the television, shook his head, and turned the set off. What good was it having thirty channels when he couldn't find anything that could keep his mind occupied? With a sigh he turned off the lights and walked down the hall to the bedroom.

After an hour he still lay staring at the ceiling. It took such an effort to keep from thinking about Libby that he couldn't get to sleep. "I give up," he said, and let images of her fill his head.

There had been some high spots in his life— the Christmas he got his first bicycle, the blue ribbon he'd won in track, Barbie Jo Britton in the backseat of his dad's Chevy, graduating from college, the day he opened the doors of his company. But none of them compared with that one single kiss tonight. Not one.

Zac sighed deeply and closed his eyes, then burrowed his head down into his pillow. He fell asleep thinking about how Libby's silky hair would feel beneath his cheek, how soft her breasts would be to touch, and her feet, those dainty sexy feet . . .

"That kiss last night really ripped it," Libby muttered as she lay Victoria on the bed and changed her diaper. The baby just blew bubbles and kicked her legs. Libby laughed. "Okay, you wiggle worm, settle down. I was all prepared to not only never hear from him again, but feel happy about it—or at least resigned to it. Why did I have to do it? Why did I think I could kiss even his cheek and get off scot-free?"

"Get off what scot-free?"

"Oh, hi, Deb," Libby said without turning around. "Did you ever think about knocking?"

"I'll think about knocking the day you start locking the front door."

"You should have knocked anyway. I could have had a hot date in here."

"Since when?" Her eyes lit up. "But then, you did have Zac Webster over for dinner last night, didn't you? How'd it go?"

Libby nodded. "Dinner went . . . fine."

"Fine," Deb repeated. "Now, I've known you for a long time, Liberty Austen, and you use that word the same way other people use the word *interesting*—to avoid committing yourself."

"That's right."

"Oh, come on. How was it?"

Libby rolled her eyes. "He came over. We ate dinner. He went home."

"Is that why you were mumbling to yourself when I came in?"

"I wasn't mumbling to myself. In case you haven't noticed, there's another person here."

"Yeah, and she's cute as a bug, but not exactly a sparkling conversationalist. And you're trying to avoid the issue."

"There *is* no issue," Libby protested. "There's just nothing to say."

"Nothing to say? You had a date with a terrific-looking guy, the same guy who delivered your baby, I might add, and you have nothing to say?"

"Okay, you want all the gory details, here they are. Victoria was fussy, the dog shed all over him, and he lit out of here about nine o'clock. Is that what you want to hear?"

"No so good, huh?"

"No so good. On a scale of one to ten, I'd have to give it an honest minus two. I don't expect I'll hear from him again. We may run into each other at Hannah's on occasion, but I think we'll wind up being cordial acquaintances more than anything else."

"And on a scale of one to ten, how would you rate the man?"

A twenty-six. "Since he coached me through

labor, that's hardly a fair question." The telephone rang. Libby handed the baby to Deb and answered it. "Hello?"

"Hello," Zac said softly. "I wanted to thank you again for dinner last night." Libby could feel that silky voice on every nerve ending in her body. She wondered if she was blushing. She wasn't the blushing sort, but she could feel heat spreading up her neck. "Um, hello. I'm glad you enjoyed it."

"How's the baby this morning?"

He always called Victoria "the baby," Libby noted, as if doing that helped him maintain a distance. "She's fine, playing with Auntie Deb."

"That's good. Since you uh, made dinner for me, I thought maybe you'd let me return the favor by taking you out to dinner."

No, I don't think that's a good idea at all. "I'd love to. When?" Shoot, she thought, it looked like her mouth had a mind of its own.

"I guess tonight would be short notice."

Libby reached out and tapped Deb on the shoulder. "If I can find a sitter tonight . . ." Deb nodded. "I can. What time."

"Seven?"

"Seven?" She looked at Deb again for approval, then said, "That would be fine. Dressy or casual?"

"I thought we'd have dinner and then perhaps go dancing afterward."

Dancing with him could be hazardous—at least to her mental health. Heaven knows, when she got near him, her brain went on leave and her hormones took over. She could handle dinner. They'd have a whole table between them and food to eat should they run out of things to talk about. But she didn't think dancing was such a good idea. "Okay. I'll see you at seven, then." Libby hung up the phone and turned to Deb, who was grinning like a Cheshire cat.

"I thought you said the date was not so good," she said slyly.

"I didn't think so."

"Apparently he thought so."

Libby turned away and fiddled with the collection of tiny perfume bottles on her dresser. "Do you want me to bring Cupcake to your place tonight, or do you want to come here?"

"I'll come here. It'll be the first time I've been out on a Saturday night in six months."

"Why?" Libby looked at Deb in surprise.

"I've sworn off men for a while. Maybe forever. I thought I told you over Easter break."

"Deb—"

"Why don't I take Victoria for a stroll so you can wash your hair or whatever in peace?"

"Okay, if you don't want to talk about it—"

"I don't." Deb turned with a toss of chestnut-brown curls. "Where's the stroller?"

"In the hall closet."

"By the way, what about feeding her?"

"She'll take a bottle with no trouble, though it probably won't be necessary. I'll nurse her just before it's time to go."

Libby spent an inordinate amount of time staring in her closet, trying to decide what to wear. She'd always liked dressing up and had been told she had a good sense of style, but any sense she had seemed to desert her as seven o'clock drew nearer.

She tried on one outfit after another and discarded all of them. One was too small since the baby, another too formal, another too casual. Finally about five minutes to seven she tugged on a white scoopneck dress that buttoned down the front.

She'd barely gotten her hair brushed into place when her bedroom door opened. Libby turned with a start. "Heavens, you scared me half to death, Deb. If you don't start knocking—"

"Hey, I just wanted to tell you Zac's here. He's waiting in the living room, trying to keep Wells from eating him alive."

"I guess I'd better go rescue him, huh?" She

looked at herself in the mirror one more time, wishing she had a butterfly net to catch all the ones fluttering inside. "Do you think this is all right?" she asked, indicating her dress.

"Perfect."

"You don't think it's a bit snug over the bust? I know I've gained at least one whole bra size since I've been nursing."

"Don't worry about it. He won't think it's too snug. But you did forget something."

"What?" Libby stared at her reflection again. "Oh, earrings." She hurriedly put on gold hoops.

"Not exactly," Deb murmured dryly. "More like shoes." She grinned and pointed at Libby's bare toes.

Libby stuffed her feet into white sandals, trying to ignore Deb's knowing look. She slicked on some lip gloss, took a deep breath, and went into the living room. It was just as well she'd taken that breath, she thought, because she didn't think she could have drawn another one had her life depended on it.

He looked terrific as usual, but that wasn't what stole her breath. It was the smile on his face that unnerved her—a smile of pure masculine appreciation. His gaze traveled from the top of her head to her feet, lingering first on the swell of her breasts, then on the tips of her toes, and the smile widened. Libby didn't know if she could stand looking at that smile the rest of the night. Not without melting into her sandals, anyway.

"You look beautiful," he murmured.

"Thank you," Libby said, feeling as if she had a mouthful of peanut butter. "You don't look so bad yourself." If he looked any better, she'd need mouth-to-mouth resuscitation.

Zac pulled a piece of paper out of his pocket and handed it to Deb. "These are the numbers where we can be reached if you need us." With a slight grimace he extricated his foot from underneath Wells, who was sitting on it, and turned to Libby. "Are you ready?"

Libby nodded, not sure she could get her tongue unstuck. She'd had her first date at fifteen and she didn't think she'd been this nervous—even though her date had been captain of the junior varsity baseball team. But then, Chris Matthews had been only cute, not sensual dynamite.

Of course the hot flashes, tight throat, and knot in her stomach could have been caused by the flu. But she didn't think so. It might have been better if she did have the flu, though. At least the flu didn't usually lead to heart involvement. Dinner with Zac could.

"Have you ever been to Wendover's?"

Libby found her voice. "No. No, I haven't, but I've heard some nice things about it."

"They specialize in seafood, but they have a few other items if you don't—"

"I love seafood."

Wendover's had a look of classic understated elegance—dark red plush carpets, pristine white tablecloths, glittering candles. And despite the Saturday night crowd, their table was private and secluded. Too secluded to Libby's way of thinking. Their whole dinner reeked of romance. And Zac was aware of it, too, if the intimate smile he turned her way was any indication.

There wasn't a lot that ever affected her appetite, but sitting across from Zac was definitely pushing it. It might have had something to do with the fact that Zac smiled at her the whole time he ate his oysters. It might have been due to the teasing comment he made about oyster's aphrodisiac qualities. It might have been. But it wasn't. It was due solely to him and the sheer male power he radiated that made every female within fifty feet—or five hundred feet—take notice.

Yet, in contrast to the previous night at her house, they talked easily. Their conversation flowed from books to movies to politics. She wasn't sure what the difference was between last night and this, but perhaps it had something to do with the deliberate charm Zac was exerting—charm so potent that she decided it either had to be a God-given talent or else he'd taken classes in it. Maybe even taught the classes.

She had a feeling that that charm was going to be overwhelming up close though, close as in dancing. And as the waiter brought their dessert, and the time to go dancing drew nearer, Libby fell into silence. This wasn't a good idea. He had a potent effect on her, but a relationship would be foolhardy. After all, she had one major drawback, at least to his way of thinking—a beautiful blue-eyed baby daughter.

As they headed to Sunny Daze for dancing, she thought she ought to tell him she had a head-ache and wanted to go home, but again her tongue seemed glued to the roof of her mouth. And she really couldn't resist one dance with him. Just one. Maybe she was flirting with trouble, but she'd never backed down from a challenge. And Zac was nothing if not a challenge.

But maybe if she got him talking about a sub-ject near and dear to his heart, he'd forget to turn that tongue-tying charm on her. And according to Hannah, the subject nearest and dearest to his heart was his company. So Libby brought up the subject. "Hannah said your company is doing quite well. I know you do something with computers, but what is it exactly?"

If Zac thought she was crazy for bringing up the subject out of the blue, at least he didn't say so as he expertly parked the car and opened her door for her. "I originally started out designing and installing customized computer programs for various businesses. I'd go into a company, look over their record keeping, talk to a number of people about what they need, and I'd personally design a software program to fit."

"Could you do that for almost any business?"

"Sure. I've done a record-keeping program for a hardware store, personnel files for a regional pharmacy chain, even a file to keep various toy designs on record. I've worked with landscaping firms, pet stores, and craft shops. Lately, though, we've begun to specialize in educational software. That seems to be the coming thing."

With his hand at her elbow he guided Libby through the crowd of people to an empty table. "Do you want something to drink?" he asked loudly over the music.

She sat down and shook her head. "No, not right now."

"Do you want to dance?"

"Not just yet. I want to hear more about your company. What is it you're working on now?"

"We've begun to concentrate more on designing educational programs to be used in schools." *God, I can't believe I'm talking shop with a woman I've been more intimate with than any other woman in my life.* And yet, except for that kiss last night, he had never touched her sexually. Not that he hadn't thought about it. He had. Over and over and over.

He didn't want to talk anymore. They'd talked constantly over dinner and he'd discovered they had things in common that he didn't want to know about. That they agreed on politics had been the final straw. One more thing in common. One more nail in his coffin.

He didn't want to have anything else in common with her. After all, not only did she have a b-a-b-y, but she had a d-o-g too. He wanted to keep this relationship purely physical. But it was damned hard when he kept finding things that drew him to her. And it was harder still when he remembered how brave, how strong she'd been during labor. And how she'd never lost her dry, sometimes wicked sense of humor—or that air of tranquility that seemed such a part of her.

He'd like to bottle the serenity that she wore like a second skin. Would she wear it when she made love—her movements calm yet thorough? Or would she discard it, like her clothes—and let sheer womanly instinct guide her in passion?

"I want to dance with you," he murmured, not caring whether or not she heard him over the loud thrum of the music. He stood and held out his hand, his gaze holding hers. "Dance with me, Libby."

SIX

Babies and dogs and happily-ever-afters, all the things that put him off, faded away when he put his arms around her. All he was conscious of was the softness of her breasts against his chest, the sway of her hips in time to the music, the swag of hair cascading down her back, the gentle friction of her thighs against his.

Her delicate scent teased him, but he couldn't put a name to it. It made him think of summer nights, sitting on his grandmother's porch swing, chasing fireflies, sipping cold lemonade, eating sugar cookies. Honeysuckle. That was it. Honeysuckle. He lay his cheek against the top of her head and breathed in the warm, sweet fragrance. It was a fragrance a man could wrap around himself.

He slipped his hands underneath her hair and

moved them up and down her back, the rough texture of the cotton on his fingertips in sharp contrast to the softness of her body beneath. He didn't want permanence, but he didn't have to live like a monk either, did he? What would be the harm in a hot, passionate, if short-term relationship? She probably didn't want to get involved either. After all, she was recently divorced.

She felt so good in his arms, though. So right. Sometimes he felt like a penniless kid with his nose pressed against a candy-store window, wanting what he can't have. A wife, two-point-five kids, a dog—one that doesn't shed—and a house with a rose garden in the back sounded nice, but he had a lot yet to do in his life.

He didn't have time for things that hadn't been planned out years in advance. He believed in plans. They hadn't let him down so far. Of course, he hadn't planned on meeting a beautiful, sexy lady with a baby and a dog. They definitely didn't fit in his agenda. But getting to know her better couldn't hurt, could it? How many more things could they have in common anyway?

He pulled back just far enough to see her face. Her eyelids fluttered, then opened. Lord, getting close was one thing, but he needed some distance right now or he was going to throw her over his shoulder and carry her out. And that would never do. He needed to demonstrate more finesse than that. Maybe some pleasant conversation would give him a chance to cool down. "You teach, right?"

She nodded, seeming surprised at his abrupt attempt at dialogue. "I teach sixth-grade English."

"I'm working on a design now for an English program aimed at sixth and seventh graders. Do you do much with computers?"

"I haven't yet, but if there was a program designed to make kids more eager to write, I'd go for it."

Zac stared at her for a moment. Damn, one more thing. "If you were going to design a program, what would you want it to do?"

"I'd want it to make kids understand that the most important skill they can develop is the skill to communicate. Everything they do from here on out, everything they become, how far they go, how they manage day-to-day life, will all depend on how well they communicate their needs."

Her voice vibrated with intensity. "Ultimately the person who goes the furthest is the one who communicates the most effectively. Just think about trying to deal with an office full of people and not knowing how to tell them precisely what you want them to do.

"When you can't get your point across concisely, you have misunderstandings, hurt feelings, and you usually wind up not getting what it was you wanted in the first place." She stopped as if just now realizing she'd been rambling on.

"I'm sorry," she murmured with a self-deprecating smile. "I'll climb down off my soap-box now. I hope I didn't put you to sleep or anything, but I have very strong feelings about that subject and can rattle on for days."

"I wasn't bored. I was just thinking how beautiful you are when you're passionate about something, and I was a little jealous that you weren't as passionate about me."

Their gazes locked and Libby swallowed hard, then ran her tongue over her bottom lip while Zac watched with avid interest. He moved his hands from her back to her waist, holding her body tight against his. His touch telegraphed a message that couldn't be mistaken. He wanted her. And he told her as much when he murmured that he wished they were alone.

Libby's eyes widened as she felt the unmistak-able surge of his lower body against hers, and she gasped. "Zac, I think we need to talk."

He spread his fingers wide over her back. "So do I, baby. But not here."

Libby started toward the table and Zac pulled

her back against him. "Don't go yet. Give me a
minute."

She didn't need to ask why he needed the time,
she could feel it. Heat suffused her whole body,
and she wondered if he could feel it radiating from
her. When she looked up at his face, she could see
him close his eyes and take a couple of deep
breaths.

"Definitely high voltage," he muttered as he
grabbed her hand and headed out the door, stopping by the table just long enough to scoop up her
purse in his other hand.

"Where are we going?"

"Not to your house yet. You're right, we do
need to talk, but I doubt we could say what needs
to be said with Deb and the baby in the other
room. And," he added dryly, "your dog lying
across my knees. We'll go to my place. We'll have
all the privacy we need."

Warning bells, beeps, and sirens went off in
her head, telling her not to go to Zac's, but she
ignored them all. Was it foolish to accompany the
lion right into his den? Probably. But she didn't
think she could have *not* gone for anything in the
world. It was dangerous to be alone with him, but
she really wanted to see where he lived, to see
what else it revealed about the man.

Neither spoke in the car. Yet they communicated as surely as if the words had been shouted. His whole body radiated hot, heady desire, hers radiated the same thing, though covered with the cloak of caution. And when they pulled up in the parking lot of his condominium, she pulled that cloak even tighter around her.

When he opened his door, he looked at her for a moment, then nodded slightly as if having made a decision. "I'll put some coffee on. Decaf. Living room is that way." He went into the kitchen.

Libby was thankful for a few minutes alone to catch her breath and credited Zac with being sensitive enough to know she needed it. She looked around the foyer, and a small frown wrinkled her forehead as she surveyed the black floor, white walls, black enameled table with black and white ceramic figurines.

She stepped into the living room and suppressed a shudder. The walls, carpet, and sofa were all white with touches of black in the throw pillows, ceramic lamps, and knickknacks. More black in the marble of the mantel over the white stone fireplace.

She knelt down in front of the octagonal fish tank and watched the black and white fish swim around. Somehow all this didn't seem like the Zac she knew—the Zac who had held her with such tenderness in the hospital, the Zac who had, when she had nearly given up, pulled her through with the sheer force of his will.

No, the Zac she knew shimmered with humor and heart and color and sound. This bland, colorless, quiet-as-a-tomb environment belonged to somebody else, somebody she didn't know. And if this was what he thought he wanted, he was kidding himself.

She poked her head into the kitchen—another black-and-white room. "What are the names of your fish?"

"The small iridescent ones are white tetras, the solid black ones are black mollies and the striped ones are angelfish."

"No, I mean what are their *names*?"

"I haven't named them." He sounded incredulous that someone should actually think he'd name fish.

Libby grimaced. She even named her houseplants. "Can I help you with anything?"

"No, I've got it all under control. It'll be another couple of minutes."

"May I use, that is, where is the—"

"First door on the right down the hall."

"Thanks." She could have cried at the unfulfilled potential of the bathroom. The skylights and greenhouse windows cried out for greenery, but all he had was one fake ficus tree in the corner next to the Jacuzzi. At least the black and white here was accented by the candy-apple-red towel tossed over the towel bar.

Had he used that towel to wipe the water from his naked body earlier as he'd stepped from a long soak in the swirling waters of the hot tub? What would it feel like to sit in there, leaning back against him, his arms around her, his hands filling themselves with her breasts?

She drew in her breath as the warm rush of desire made her breasts tingle. Or were they tingling because it had been nearly four hours since she'd nursed Victoria? Sighing, she stuffed a couple of tissues in the cups of her bra just in case they leaked.

She couldn't resist peeking into Zac's bedroom to see if it too, was the horrible black-and-white, only to find a pleasant surprise. The luxurious carpet provided a wickedly thick pearl-gray background to the fire-engine red bedspread and curtains. A crowded bookshelf took up one whole wall, old movie posters another, and photographs covered the other two. She smiled to herself. Now, this was the Zac she knew.

Libby stepped inside to get a closer look. When the heels of her sandals sank two inches into the carpet, she couldn't resist taking them off and letting her toes wriggle in the plush fibers.

"Here's your coffee."

Libby jumped and turned around, embarrassed at having been caught snooping. But Zac didn't seem to mind. He simply handed her the cup and pointed to a picture of an attractive dark-haired man and a willowy blond.

"This is my brother Matt and his wife Alice. And this is Ben." Zac indicated a photograph of a younger Hannah looking adoringly at a tall, dark, rather dangerous-looking man. "It was taken just a few months before they separated."

There was a picture of the three brothers together, all wearing cutoffs and standing in front of a lake, Ben on one side of Zac, Matt on the other.

"And this picture?" Libby pointed to a photo showing a definitely panic-stricken Zac staring down at a baby in one arm and a toddler in the other.

"Gee, they don't seem to be screaming or anything."

"They started wailing about two minutes after that picture was taken," Zac said dryly, then added in a totally different tone of voice, "I've thought a lot about getting you into my bedroom. I just didn't think we'd be discussing old photos at the time."

That reminded Libby of why they were there. "Yeah, well, I think we should take our coffee back into the living room and talk." When she noticed Zac seemed to be staring with utter fascination at her feet, she curled her toes into the carpet.

"You may be right," he said in a strangled voice. "Why don't we go into the living room?"

Whose bright idea was it to talk anyway? Zac stared at the steaming cup of coffee clutched in his hand. "So what do you want to talk about?" he finally asked after several uncomfortable minutes of silence.

Libby carefully set her nearly full cup on the table and clenched her hands together in her lap. "I think you know. About you and me. Um, us. Our relationship. If we have one—"

"We do." Zac emphasized the words. "I can't think of anything I'd rather discuss than our relationship. And how to advance it."

"That's what I want to talk about. Zac, this is only our third date."

"So? A lot of relationships have begun on even less than three dates."

"I still think things are moving too fast."

"Maybe. But then, we didn't exactly get to know each other in your usual run-of-the-mill way either. We learned more important things about each other during your labor than most people learn about each other in weeks of dinners and movies."

He leaned back on the sofa and stretched out his legs, looking comfortable. Libby only wished she could feel as at ease, much less look it. She knew she had twisted her hands together in her lap—she usually did when she got nervous. And Zac made her so nervous that it was a wonder she hadn't tied her fingers in knots—or a hangman's noose.

"But we still don't *know* each other. Going through labor gave us a sense of intimacy that makes us feel as if—as if—"

"As if we should be more heavily involved than we are."

"Right."

"Have you stopped to think that these feelings might be right?"

"Have you stopped to think that they might not?" Libby fell silent for a moment, trying to put her feelings in words, then continued slowly. "If those feelings were right, then I'd feel better about becoming—becoming—"

"Intimate."

She felt a moment of pique that he'd finished a sentence of hers for the second time. On the other hand, she wasn't doing such a great job of finishing them herself. She sighed. "Right. Intimate.

But my head is saying that we really don't know each other yet."

"I can't imagine a better way to get to know each other than by making love."

"Physically, maybe, but not mentally. And not emotionally."

"Oh, for Pete's sake!" Zac sighed in exasperation. "I know you. I know you like science fiction, murder mysteries, dogs, plants, and Italian food. You like pre-Columbian art and orchids. You like old movies, you wax eloquent about teaching kids, you're a political liberal and an economic conservative."

"But, Zac, you still don't know me. I could hate dogs and little kids for all you know."

He looked at her with one eyebrow raised. "Yeah. Right."

"There are plenty of other things you don't know too. I might be a really horrible person or something."

Zac sighed. "So tell me something really horrible you've done."

"Well, I—I . . ." She stopped for a moment, then snapped her fingers. "I know. I cheated on a test once."

"Mmm-hmm. And how old were you at the time?"

Libby looked down at her hands and mumbled something.

"What? I didn't quite catch that."

"I said, I was eight. Satisfied?"

"God, we have a real criminal element here, don't we?"

"But we could," Libby said earnestly. "Don't you see?"

"So tell me something, Libby. Tell me something about yourself that I really need to know."

"I'm impatient. And I can be, um, obstinate, on occasion."

"I'd already figured that one out," he murmured dryly. "And I'm both of those things too. So tell me something I don't know."

"Zac, this is silly."

"You think so? Let me tell you something, Libby. We know each other better than you think. We went through an incredible experience together. And you learn a lot about people during things like that. I already know you better than I knew most of the women I've been involved with."

He flashed a sudden grin. "So what do you need to know about me—besides the fact that I'm an all-around great guy?"

"How about your favorite color?" Libby ventured cautiously, though she really wanted to know more about those other women.

"Red."

After seeing his bedroom and his fire-engine-red BMW, that came as no surprise. "I sort of suspected as much. Then why is most of your apartment done in black and white?"

Zac looked less comfortable than he had a minute earlier. "I told the decorator I wanted something clean and uncluttered-looking, and this is what she came up with."

"Do you like it?" Libby watched him thoughtfully. He couldn't possibly like this sterile, static environment.

"Of course!" There was a defiant tone to his voice. "I find it very—er—uncluttered. Let's get back to the subject at hand. You already know my favorite books, food, and movies. Your politics agree with mine, and you know I also like pre-Columbian art. And you know my favorite color. What else do you need to know?"

Libby smiled. "What's your favorite food?"

"Need you ask?"

"Italian?"

"Bingo. Shrimp scampi, to be exact, though I also have a soft spot for fettuccine Alfredo. Anything else you need to know? My life's an open book."

"What's your hobby?"

"What do you mean, what's my hobby?"

"What do you do for fun?" Libby asked.

Zac stopped. For fun? He finally said, "I play handball four times a week with Ryan Miller. He's my vice president." But was that really fun? he thought. He did it because he knew he had a sedentary job and it helped him keep in shape. When was the last time he really did anything because he enjoyed it?

"What do *you* do for fun?" He'd turn the tables on her. *Let's see if you find it so easy to answer.*

"I read, I garden. I rent old sci-fi movies and huddle down with potato chips and onion dip. I also ride my bicycle."

"I have a bike." Of course he hadn't ridden it in fifteen years, but it probably still worked. They didn't usually fall to pieces of old age, did they?

"Maybe we can meet over at the park sometime and ride together." Libby gave him an ingenuous smile.

"Maybe." Was it true that you never forgot how to ride a bike? He hoped so. He liked the idea of cuddling down with her in front of an old sci-fi movie better, though. With any luck at all, they'd not only miss most of the movie, they'd crush the potato chips. And he could think of some real interesting things to do with the onion dip. "Now, back to the excuses you're trying to find for us not to go to bed together—"

"How about I don't do casual sex?"

Zac gave her a look as hot and strong as black coffee. "Baby, I doubt sex between us would be casual. It would be hot and sweaty and intense."

"I'm sure it would," Libby murmured almost without thinking. "But it would still be a short-term, here-and-now thing. I want more than that."

"What do you want, Libby?" He reached out and snared a strand of her hair, twirling it around the end of his finger. "Happily ever after? The prince on the white horse?"

"Maybe. What's the matter with that?"

"You'll be waiting a long time."

"You don't believe in love and marriage?"

"I'm not sure if love exists or not. Marriage does, but who's to say it's a good thing?"

"People who are happily married might disagree with you."

"Who's happily married? Look at Hannah and you. And Deb."

"How about your brother and his wife? From the pictures, they look happy."

"They seem to be, but how do we know it'll last?"

Libby shrugged. "How do you know it won't? There are just some things you have to take on faith. If you go into marriage with the attitude that it's a temporary thing and you can always get out of it, maybe you're not inclined to work hard at it."

"And did you work at it?"

Libby looked straight at him with eyes as clear and blue as a summer sky. "With everything that was in me. We started seeing a marriage counselor after the first year of marriage. When Bobby decided it wasn't his problem and stopped going, I continued to see the counselor on my own. And even when I left Bobby, I did it, hoping to shock him into seeing what was happening to our marriage."

"Do you still love him?"

She shook her head. "No. That died somewhere between the second and third year of our marriage. About the time he'd lost his seventh or eighth job, about the time that he'd been through his third or fourth girlfriend. But if he had been willing to try to work things out, I probably would have."

"But you still believe that happy marriages exist."

"I've seen a few. My parents, my grandparents, numerous aunts and uncles."

"But you're not going to wait forever for the knight in shining armor, are you? They just don't exist."

"Maybe they do, maybe they don't." *And some-*

times, maybe they stand by you during labor and deliver your baby. "Anyway, I have a baby now. I have to think about setting an example for my daughter. She's going to notice everything I do."

"I hardly think a two-month-old baby is noticing examples," Zac said.

"Zac, you're not listening to what I'm saying."

"I'm listening."

"No, you're *hearing* it, but you're not listening to it. Maybe this isn't such a good idea. Maybe I should go home now. It's getting late, anyway." She looked around. "Where's my purse?"

Zac leaned even farther back on the sofa, managing not to wince as the clasp of her purse dug into the small of his back. "Gee, I don't know. Did you leave it in the bathroom?"

She continued to look around the room. "No, I could've sworn— There it is." She pointed to the strap showing from beneath his thigh.

Zac watched her with an all-too-innocent look. "If you want it, here it is."

Libby stared at his come-and-get-it-I-dare-you smile and a mischievous smile lit her own face. "You don't think I'll do it, do you?"

"I don't think you've got the nerve." Zac's eyes laughed at her as he tucked the strap all the way under his leg.

Libby pursed her lips, difficult to do with the wide smile pulling at them, and tilted her head to one side. She got up from the white leather chair she'd been sitting in and stepped over to the sofa. With her arms crossed in front of her, she made a big production of observing Zac from all sides, as if trying to decide the best method by which to obtain her objective. With a wicked gleam in her eye she made a sudden jab at one side of his ribs with her fingers.

He jumped and she giggled, poking a finger at the other side. When he twisted to one side to avoid her, she grabbed her purse from behind him.

"Hey, no fair," he exclaimed with a laugh. "You play dirty."

"I do, don't I?" she agreed smugly. Heavens, what a laugh he had. Full-bodied and contagious, it contained an intimate invitation to join in.

"I can play dirty too," he murmured, and hooked an arm around her waist, tugging her down into his lap. When she laughingly struggled, he wrapped both arms around her and held her in place. "I suggest you stop squirming," he warned her.

"Why should I?"

"Well . . ." His voice trailed off and his gaze held hers in a meaningful look as a slow, wicked grin spread over his face. "You can keep on wiggling if you want to, but you'll have to take responsibility for any consequences." He settled her more securely on his lap, where he knew she could feel his growing arousal.

Libby immediately stilled. "Let me up, Zac."

"Please." His voice caressed the word as he said it.

"Please let me up."

"In a minute. Right now I want to enjoy the way you feel."

Libby knew exactly how she felt. She felt hot. Heat spread like an epidemic throughout her body, and again she wondered if her never-blushing cheeks were doing just that, because her face burned. And it burned even hotter when his hands brushed the outside of her breasts, then slid around to cup them.

"I've wanted to do this since the car. Do you remember?" he whispered.

Heaven help her, she'd never forget.

"I've wanted to see if you were really as full and soft as you seemed." He gently squeezed her breasts, closing his eyes as if to savor the pleasure it brought. "You are. Even more than I dreamed."

"Zac, you should stop this," she protested

weakly, but he rested his lips against hers, swallowing her protest.

"Maybe I should, but I don't think I can," he murmured against her mouth, and unbuttoned the top button of her dress. He undid the next button and ran the back of his hand down inside along the lacy edge of her bra.

Libby wriggled on his lap again, this time oblivious of the physical effect it was having on him, too caught up in the physical effect he was having on her. "Zac," she breathed. "I don't know about this."

"I do," he muttered hoarsely. "Leave it all to me." He unbuttoned a third button on her dress, then a fourth, and slid his hands underneath the bodice of her dress to unhook her bra. When the clasp popped free, he splayed his hands over the smooth skin of her back, his fingers pressing into the soft flesh. Her eyelids fluttered, then closed, and Zac bent his head down to hers.

It might have been easier to say no had he tried a deep, passionate kiss right away, but he didn't. Instead, he outlined her mouth with the tip of his tongue, nibbled at the fullness of her bottom lip, then nipped her chin lightly before leaving a trail of warm kisses along her jaw to her ear.

He took her earlobe between his teeth and toyed with the gold hoop a moment before nuzzling his way back to her waiting mouth. There he moved his lips over hers in a kiss of the gentlest persuasion, but one that would take only the fullest surrender.

With a faint moan—of protest? of capitulation?—Libby opened her mouth to his and his tongue swirled in, over and around hers. Her hands fastened on his shoulders and her head slowly fell back, inviting him to investigate the creamy-smooth skin of her throat, which he did with exacting thoroughness.

He pressed hungry kisses along her collarbone, then along the swell of her breasts, while his hands smoothed the dress from her shoulders. Funny, he found himself thinking hazily, not only did her skin have the smoothness of cream, it tasted like it—rich, sweet. Addictive.

Her dress fell to her waist and Zac slid the satin straps of her lacy bra down her arms, following behind with his lips. When her bra, too, dropped away, Zac moved his lips to taste this new territory, only he got a mouthful of tissue.

"Wha—?"

His exclamation was like a cold wind blowing away the fog that had engulfed Libby's reason, and she froze for one brief moment before hastily pulling up her dress and sliding from Zac's lap.

To her relief, Zac didn't try to stop her, but he

did keep an arm around her shoulders. She could feel the deep, steadying breaths he drew in—or was it her? "How'd I get the tissue in my mouth?" he finally asked with the faintest twinkle in his eye.

Heavens, she was mortified! She knew she had to be blushing this time. She muttered, "I stuffed it in my bra in case I leaked."

"In case what leaked?" Zac looked mystified, then his face suddenly cleared as awareness dawned. "Oh. Does that happen often?"

Libby didn't meet his eyes as she hastily put herself to rights. "Almost never now, but it did the first three or four weeks. Sometimes even hearing the cry of a baby on television triggered it."

"Must be inconvenient."

"It can be when it happens. It can be really embarrassing. Like I said, it almost never happens now, though." She was rambling and she knew it. "I just didn't want to take any chances," she finished lamely. Libby buttoned her top button and stood, brushing her hands down the front of her dress.

"So what triggered it this time?"

"I don't know. I was just thinking about you and—" she stopped dead. With any luck at all, maybe he hadn't heard what she said. She watched as a self-satisfied smile curved his lips. No such luck. Well, with this indecently thick white carpet, maybe she could just hide between the fibers. "I think it's about time I went home."

"If that's what you want." Zac stood, still smiling, though he didn't comment on her verbal slip. "Don't worry, Libby, you're safe. For now anyway. But I'm not going to stop, baby. I think we know each other plenty well. And I know you well enough to know I want you. I want you a helluva lot."

"Is wanting enough for you?"

"It has to be. I don't have time for wives and kids and picket fences for a few years yet. And I doubt I'll ever have time for kids. They take too much—too much time, too much energy. Anyway, kids and I don't get along."

"I'll consider myself warned," Libby quipped lightly, though her heart sank at his words. "Although maybe you should consider yourself warned too. I can be very persuasive. And I think you and kids could eventually get along just fine."

"Then I'll look forward to you *trying* to persuade me. It could get very interesting."

Libby looked at him for a moment, then said soberly, "Is it worth pursuing, Zac?"

"A relationship?"

She nodded. "We're so different. You don't

like kids and I have a daughter. You don't want to marry anytime soon, and I believe in marriage."

"Even after Bobby."

"Even after Bobby. It's not marriage that was the problem between him and me; it was that Bobby wasn't ready for it yet."

"I'm not either."

"Maybe not. That's why I want to know if it's worth pursuing."

Zac fell silent as he appeared to consider the question. "There's something special between us, Libby. Something compelling enough that I think it ought to be explored. I really want to see you again."

"I—I don't know. I need some time to think. Can you take me home now?"

Silence reigned again as he drove her home and, as on the way to his apartment, it was a silence full of the unspoken. Only this time, instead of awareness, it was swimming with confusion, wariness, and frustration.

"You don't have to see me to the door," Libby said when he pulled into her driveway.

"I wouldn't do it any other way." He took her elbow as they headed up the sidewalk. "I'll call you tomorrow."

She shook her head. "Give it some time, okay? Give me some time."

In answer, Zac pulled her to him and devoured her mouth in a deep, drugging kiss. Like a hurricane, he stormed in and laid siege to her senses with swirling caresses and torrential kisses. He pulled away. "That's all the time you're going to get." He released her suddenly and stalked off to his car, leaving her shaky and weak. If she hadn't been holding on to the door frame, she'd have fallen to her knees. The only consolation she had was knowing that his face looked as shattered as she felt.

SEVEN

He called the next day, as he'd promised, only he caught Libby in the middle of Victoria's bath time, so she didn't have time to say more than a few words while she struggled to hang on to a slippery, squirming baby.

In the clear light of day, with her now-dry and sleepy daughter snuggled in her arms, she felt better about her decision to cool things a bit with Zac. It didn't help her resolve to hear him on the phone, though. One word in that soft voice and her resolve—as well as her knees—turned to oatmeal.

He was so persuasive, so compelling, that every time she heard his voice she could feel it pulling her as surely as if he were a magnet and she were a piece of iron. When he called her later that afternoon, Libby found herself making an excuse not to talk. She had a feeling Zac knew it was an excuse.

He called back at nine that evening. "Um, I was just putting the baby to bed, so this isn't a good time," Libby said.

There was a long pause on the other end of the line. "Should I make an appointment to call back?" he asked in exasperation.

"Look, Zac, I told you last night, I wanted some time. We want two different things out of a relationship. You want—"

"Hot sex?"

"Would you please stop finishing my sentences for me? But, yes, that's what you want. I want more. I want a future. And right now I'm not sure whether I can risk a relationship with you— with any man—who can't give me that."

"This isn't over between us, baby, not by a long shot. But if you want time, then you've got it. I just can't guarantee how much I'm going to give you." The line went dead as he hung up the phone and Libby sighed with relief. And with regret.

Zac called her two days later. He asked about the baby and mentioned an all-night sci-fi film festival that was going to be on television Friday. Libby expected him to ask her to watch it with him and had excuses all ready, only he didn't ask. When she hung up the phone, she flopped down on the sofa and stared at Victoria. "How do you like that?" she muttered to the baby, who sucked her pacifier and kicked her feet in the air.

"I'm so confused. I tell him to give me some space, and when he does, I'm not happy about it. What would you do, Cupcake? What would you do?"

Victoria accidentally caught her finger in her pacifier and pulled it out of her mouth. After a surprised look, she began to whimper. Libby gave a sympathetic sigh and replaced the pacifier. "I know exactly how you feel."

By Friday night, when Zac hadn't called again, Libby was toying with the idea of calling him. She considered him a friend, she reasoned with herself. He had delivered her baby. Certainly that gave them some ties. What was wrong with one friend calling another?

She quickly dialed his number before she could change her mind, but all she got was his answering machine. She felt an unreasoning anger as she hung up the receiver—a little harder than necessary. For all his talk about "something between them," it hadn't taken him long to find a date for Friday night.

After she'd put Victoria down to sleep, she

decided to forego the usual chips and dip for a pint of ice cream, her favorite comfort food. Ordinarily, she would have had double Dutch chocolate, but since chocolate seemed to give Victoria colic, she settled for French vanilla. It was so calorie-rich, she could almost feel the weight settle on her hips. If she gained ten pounds, she was going to blame nobody but Zac.

About fifteen minutes before the first science fiction movie came on, the phone rang.

Libby picked up the receiver. "Hello?" For a moment Libby couldn't hear anything but the sound of a baby's agitated cries, then she heard a muffled "Libby?"

"Zac?"

"Libby, I need help!" he said desperately. "Nicky's been screaming two hours straight, and I don't know what to do."

"Have you fed him?"

"Yes, and I burped him and I've changed him and I've walked the floor the past hour with him. Libby, you've got to help me. I'm going deaf in one ear and Hannah's damn cat is starting to snarl at me every time I walk by it."

"What do you want me to do?"

"What? I can't hear you over the baby. Can you speak up?"

DON'T HOLD BACK!

1. **No obligation!** No purchase necessary! Enter our Sweepstakes for a chance to win!
2. **FREE!** Get your first shipment of 6 Loveswept books, *and* a lighted makeup case as a free gift.
3. **Save money!** Become a member and about once a month you get 6 books for the price of 4! Return any shipment you don't want.
4. **Be the first!** You'll always receive your Loveswept books before they are available in stores. You'll be the first to thrill to these exciting new stories.

Give in to love and see where passion leads you!
Enter the Winners Classic Sweepstakes and
send for your FREE lighted makeup case and
6 FREE Loveswept books today!

(See details inside.)

Libby spoke louder. "What do you want me to do?"

"Can you come over to Hannah's and help me figure out what to do? Please, Libby, I'm getting desperate."

"Where's Hannah?"

She heard a crash over the phone and the word *cat* bordered on either side by curses. "What?" he yelled into the phone.

The questions had better wait until later. "I'll be there as soon as I can." She stared at the phone for a moment after she'd replaced the receiver. Zac hadn't sounded this harried in the hospital— not even when he'd delivered her baby.

Libby hurriedly exchanged her robe for jeans and a T-shirt. She put the baby in the car seat, thankful that she hadn't awakened; Victoria had been fretful earlier that evening.

She'd been to Hannah's only once since they'd met in the Lamaze class, but didn't have any trouble finding it. After she turned onto Peterson Street, all she had to do was look for Zac's bright red BMW.

The front door opened as soon as she got out of her car and Zac strode out. "Thank God you could get here. I hope he's not sick or anything. He just keeps yelling."

She unfastened Victoria from the car seat and

handed her to Zac. "Hold her while I get her things."

Zac stared down at the quietly sleeping baby lying in his outstretched hands. "Uh, Libby? I don't think this is such a good idea."

"Nonsense. You'll do fine. We need to work on the way you're holding her, though, but let me go check on Nicky first."

Hoisting the diaper bag, Libby headed into the house, leaving Zac to follow, still holding the baby out in front of him. As soon as she walked in the door, she was assailed by the frantic cries coming from the bassinet in the corner.

She went straight to the baby. Poor thing. She felt his head. He was flushed and sweaty, but that wasn't from a fever. It was partly from crying, mostly because he was bundled so snugly.

"Why do you have so many covers on him?" Libby asked as she removed two baby blankets. "Good heavens! Zac, you've dressed him in a flannel snowsuit! What in the world were you thinking of?" She unsnapped the fuzzy garment and removed it. Already the baby's cries were sounding less shrill.

"He wet all over his other thing," Zac said defensively. "I just put him in the first thing I grabbed out of the drawer. Is he all right?"

"I think he's fine." She picked Nicky up and

put him on her shoulder. She cooed to him for a few minutes and patted his back, and he quieted down. Within a few more minutes he was nodding against her neck. When Libby carried him to his room to tuck him in, Zac sat on the sofa, Victoria still straddled across his hands.

He stared down at the baby. She looked like a doll in a pink romper. She was making little sucking motions with her lips, even in her sleep, and her long doll-like eyelashes fluttered. Zac felt a funny clutching in his chest. Could've been indigestion, he supposed, but he was afraid it was something else, something that could change his life completely.

Libby came out of the baby's room, shutting the door behind her. "I think he'll sleep for a while. Now, tell me how you wound up baby-sitting? Hannah must have used pretty heavy guns to get you to agree."

"You want to take the baby?" he asked hopefully, but she made no move to. Instead, she sat in the chair next to the sofa and crossed her legs. He couldn't help but spend a moment appreciating the way the soft, faded denim molded itself to her long, well-shaped legs. Then his gaze fell to the snug leather boots hugging her slim ankles. Nice. Sexy. Not as sexy as her dainty bare toes, but sexy nonetheless. He wondered if she still had that pink polish on her toenails?

"Hannah had to drive into Pittsburgh to talk to someone about Homebodies—you know, the errand-running and shopping service she's starting up. Then she wanted to meet an old sorority sister for dinner and asked if I'd sit with Nicky. She said he'd probably sleep, but if he woke up, all I'd have to do was give him a bottle, burp him, and he'd go right back to sleep. He didn't."

"Well, he's okay now and almost asleep. But there's something you might want to keep in mind for future baby-sitting jobs—"

"I don't intend for there to be any more!" he said with such vehemence that Victoria started. He stared down at her, hardly daring to breathe, while she moved her arms and sighed, apparently deciding whether or not to wake up. When she settled back down, he continued. "I told you, I'm no good with kids. I don't know why I ever thought I could do this."

"It might help if you held the baby right."

"What's wrong with the way I'm holding her?"

"She's not exactly a sack of potatoes, Zac. Babies need to feel safe and secure. If that's the way you've been holding Nicky, it's no wonder he's been screaming bloody murder. Hold her close to you, like this." She showed him how to nestle the baby next to his chest. "Now wrap your other arm around her too. See?"

He cradled Victoria in his arms and looked down at her with such an intense expression on his face that Libby inexplicably felt tears sting her eyes. Why couldn't he realize how natural he looked cuddling a baby in his arms. Cuddling *her* baby.

"Like this?"

"Just like that." Libby said softly.

Zac smiled. "This doesn't seem so hard. You hold them next to you the way you'd hold a football when you're running to the end zone."

Libby rolled her eyes. "Right. I take it you played high school football?"

"One year of junior varsity, two years of varsity, and a year of college ball."

"Why only a year in college?"

"I'd gone to college on an academic scholarship and football took up too much time."

The telephone let out a sharp jangle. "Grab that, would you?" Zac said hurriedly. "God, I hope it doesn't wake up Nicky."

Libby stepped into the kitchen for a moment, then poked her head back around the edge of the door. "It's Hannah."

"Tell her everything's fine and find out what time she'll be home," Zac said.

"He said to tell you everything's fine and find out what time you'll be home," Libby repeated into the phone.

"I'll be home about midnight. Are you sure everything's okay? Why are you there?"

"Um, Zac, he thought I might want to come by and watch the sci-fi film fest on TV tonight."

"Where is he anyway?"

"He's on the sofa with Victoria."

"Holding her?" Hannah sounded incredulous.

"Holding her."

"There might be hope for him yet, hmm?"

"Maybe. Are you having a good time?"

"Great," Hannah said enthusiastically. "I'll call you tomorrow and tell you about it. I think I'm really going to be able to get my business off the ground. I really do. It'll be the first thing I've ever accomplished completely on my own. I'll see you in a couple of hours."

"What time will she be home?" Zac asked the minute Libby came back into the living room.

"She said around midnight."

"Oh. Nicky'll probably stay asleep. Don't you think?"

"Probably." Libby looked down at her hands, then looked back up with a bright smile. "I guess I'd better go, then. Nicky's fine and—"

"Please stay."

"Zac—"

"That film festival is on, you know. We could watch it together, like you told Hannah."

"I don't know."

"*Jupiter's Moon* comes on in a few minutes," Zac said slyly. "I seem to remember you saying that was one of your favorites. If you leave now, you'll miss the first part of it."

"I guess I could stay."

"What do you want to do with the baby?"

Libby's eyebrows went up. "You mean you're not dying to hold her all night?"

"I could hold her for a few more minutes while you fix a place for her to sleep. Hannah wouldn't mind if you used the bassinet over there."

"She looks good in your arms," Libby said wistfully as she went over to straighten the covers in the bassinet.

"Don't get any ideas."

"Hey, I was just stating a fact," she said over her shoulder.

"*You'd* look great in my arms."

"Zac—"

He sighed in exasperation. "Sorry." There was silence for a moment, then Zac muttered, "Damn!"

"What's wrong?"

"My pants leg suddenly feels warm and wet. Does that give you a clue?"

Libby grimaced. "I'm sorry. Here, give her to me."

"With great pleasure." He handed the baby to Libby and looked down at the large dark spot on his khaki trousers. He headed into the kitchen to get a paper towel. Or maybe a whole handful.

Libby changed Victoria and was tucking her in the bassinet when Zac came back into the room. She could see where Zac had apparently stuffed paper towels in his trouser leg to keep the damp fabric off his thigh. Libby bit back a grin at his disgruntled look.

"I don't have anything to change into, so this will have to do." He sat back down on the sofa and held out a hand to her. "Come here."

"Um, isn't it about time for the movie?" Libby hedged, going to the television and fiddling with the dials. "What channel? Oh, here it is." The screen showed the opening credits.

"So come here and sit down with me to watch it."

"I think the view is better from over here." She indicated a soft blue velour recliner.

"The view is great from here," Zac said with appreciation as he watched the denim pull tight over her bottom as she bent over to tug at her boot. "If your feet hurt, feel free to take off your boots." *Please*.

"Thanks. How'd you know my feet hurt?"

He hadn't. He'd only hoped. "Well, the boots look kind of new," he ventured.

"They are new and the leather hasn't had a chance to give yet." She sat on the edge of the chair and tugged at one.

"Let me." Zac knelt in front of the chair and took a deep breath. Only sliding her panties off could have been sexier, he thought as he gently slid off one boot and laid it aside. With iron control he kept his hands from shaking as he massaged her foot through the sock for a moment.

"Mmm, nice," she murmured.

He removed the other boot and massaged that foot, then slipped the sock off. He gently cradled her foot in his hand and rubbed the tension away, massaging each toe, then her instep, then her heel.

God, she had beautiful feet—slim and dainty, her well-manicured toenails painted shell-pink. "Have you ever worn red nail polish?" he found himself asking, vaguely surprised at the husky sound to his voice. His fingers lingered on her feet in a gentle caress.

Libby had closed her eyes in pleasure and

opened them again at his question. "Why do you ask?"

"Just curious," he said. "I happen to think red nail polish is very attractive." He lightly ran his fingers over the sole of her foot. When she shivered in response, he did it again. She was ticklish. Not a lot, but enough to be sexy.

"The movie is coming on," she said, her voice the least bit unsteady.

"Do you want me to stop?" He ran his fingers over the other foot, desire coiling like an overwound watch in his stomach.

"No. Yes, I mean, I don't want to miss the movie."

"If that's what you want." His fingers lingered a moment, then he stood, turning quickly so she wouldn't see the heavy arousal pressing against his zipper. What was there about those slender little feet that made him long to get his hands on them— or on her?

"Come sit next to me on the sofa," he urged. "Just for a little while."

"I really ought to go check on the babies."

"They'll let you know if they need anything. Babies are good at that."

"Maybe a snack—"

"Come here, Libby." He held out his hand. Slowly, almost reluctantly, she walked over to the sofa and put her hand in his. He tugged gently, and she sat next to him on the sofa. "This isn't such a good idea," she whispered. "You know what happens when we—when we—"

"Get too close?"

"You're finishing my sentences again," she complained, but smiled as she said it.

"Nothing will happen that you don't want. You know that." He twisted his body slightly so he could see her face.

"Zac, I've always wanted whatever happened to happen. That doesn't stop me from genuinely believing that it's not a good idea. At least not while we're poles apart in our thinking." She looked up to find him watching her, then looked back down at her hands, vaguely surprised to find them twisted together in her lap.

"Our bodies aren't poles apart."

"No, I'd say they're more like an inch or so apart. But our wants are."

"What I *want* is you. And you want me too. You know you do."

"I don't want to discuss what you or I want. I want to discuss what I *don't* want. And I don't want to discuss this anymore."

"You want to try repeating that?" Zac said with a grin.

"No." She couldn't help smiling back. "I want to watch the movie."

Zac took a deep breath. "If that's what you want, then your wish is my command." He sat back and draped a casual arm around her shoulder, pulling her back to rest against him. He made no further move.

After a few minutes Libby cast a suspicious glance in his direction. He merely met her gaze with a beatific smile. "Great movie."

Libby turned her attention back to the television. So he had backed down as she'd asked. She wasn't sure whether she was relieved—or miserable.

They sat, side by side, watching the movie in companionable silence. Even though part of Libby was disappointed that he hadn't continued to try to seduce her, part of her appreciated his thoughtfulness in giving her the time she believed might make things clearer.

Unfortunately, the more time she spent with Zac, the less clear things became. He didn't have to touch her at all for the physical attraction to get in the way. All she had to do was hear his rough-soft voice or feel his chocolate-brown gaze on her. And lacking his presence, her imagination did an outstanding job of thinking of these things on its own.

Sitting next to him on the sofa was stretching her imagination to the limits. She was acutely aware of his arm around her and the way the fingers of his hand brushed her collarbone. Her imagination took it a step—or two—further and had those same strong hands stroking her breasts, sliding down over her stomach, cupping her bottom.

Even in the first flush of her youthful infatuation with Bobby she'd never felt like this. Libby drew in a deep breath, wriggled slightly, and tried to focus her attention on the movie. But it wasn't easy when she could see only the mist of desire in front of her.

"Something wrong?" Zac turned to look at her.

That's when she made her mistake. She turned her head and met his gaze head-on. When she saw the hunger displayed so blatantly in his eyes, she was lost. How could she fight the unfightable? How could she stop the unstoppable? With a sigh she surrendered gracefully to fate.

Zac ran his free hand down the side of her face, then laced his fingers through her hair. He lowered his head to hers and kissed one corner of her mouth, then the other. He kissed the tip of her nose, each eyelid, and pressed a trail of kisses along her jaw. But he didn't take her lips until Libby brought up her hands and threaded her fingers imperiously through his thick mahogany waves and opened her mouth to his.

With a groan he swept in, his tongue dueling and dancing with hers while he pressed her closer. He tugged her T-shirt free of her jeans and ran hungry hands over her back, then around front to cup her breasts through the sleek fabric of her bra.

When his thumbs found her sensitive nipples, she made a low sound in the back of her throat—a sound he caught with his mouth and echoed back to her. With a single snap he unfastened her bra and pulled it up to expose her breasts to his seeking hands. Libby shivered and closed her eyes. She didn't want this, yet she'd never wanted anything more. And more than anything, she wanted to touch him. She needed to touch him.

She smoothed her hands over the front of his maroon sweatshirt, the soft cotton teasing her fingertips. His sharply indrawn breath encouraged her to explore further, and she let her hands roam over his broad, muscled chest, relishing the slight give of his firm muscles.

But soon even that contact wasn't enough. She wanted more. Zac seemed to know what she wanted, and he released her just long enough to impatiently tug his sweatshirt free of his trousers and over his head, tossing it on the floor. He took her hands and placed the palms flat on his chest. "Yes. Touch me, baby," he whispered. "Touch me too."

He looked down and watched her hands glide over his chest, circling through the crisp curls of hair. He pressed her hand to him. "Feel my heart beat, Libby. Feel it race."

Wordlessly, she did the same to him, showing him that her heart beat every bit as hard and as fast as his. Then she took her hands and ran them both back over his chest, covering each flat nipple with her palm. He reached out and did the same to her, cupping her breasts in his hands for a moment before laying his palms over her nipples. "Show me how you want me to touch you," he whispered hoarsely.

Libby circled her thumbs around his nipples, then waited as he did the same to hers. She wasn't leaking, she thought with vague surprise as she slid her hands to his shoulders and held on for dear life.

Slowly Zac eased her back on the sofa until her head rested against the arm. He kissed her breasts one at a time, then his lips traced a path down to the button at the waist of her jeans. He tried to slide it undone but couldn't. "Damn button-front jeans," he muttered with breathless humor against the skin of her stomach.

Libby squeaked out, "Sorry."

"Don't ever wear them again," he ordered huskily as he managed to work the button open, then started on the next. The last button undone, Zac slid his hand inside the waist of her jeans and ran his fingers around the lacy edge of her bikini panties.

"Zac." Her voice was a breathy whisper, a plea for him to end this torment—and to never stop.

He answered the plea by sliding his hand over the smooth skin of her stomach to the downy curls that guarded her womanly secrets. Libby arched her hips against his questing fingers. "You're so hot, so sweet," he groaned, and proceeded to investigate further.

An ear-splitting scream broke the silence, and Libby stiffened. "Victoria." She scrambled to sit up, then fumbled with her bra and blouse before hurrying to pick up the crying baby. Zac sat up, dropping his head into his hands, but only for a moment, as Victoria's cries were answered by a sudden wail from the bedroom. "Damn," Zac muttered. He tugged on his sweatshirt and went to get his nephew.

It was as if the room had been wired for stereo. The babies cried in unison for the next half hour. Zac and Libby passed each other in the middle of the floor as they paced back and forth, wailing babies on their shoulders. No sooner had they gotten one baby quiet than the other would let out a howl and the first baby would join back in. Finally they managed to get them both quiet at the same time. Nicky gave a big toothless smile, burped, and spit up on his uncle's sweatshirt.

Libby had to grin as first shock, then realization, then pure and utter disgust registered on Zac's face. It was just as well that Libby couldn't make out what Zac muttered as he put Nicky in the bassinet and stalked into the kitchen.

A few minutes later he was back with a huge wet spot on his sweatshirt. "I swear, it's like a conspiracy or something," he complained mildly when he came back into the living room. "Last time I saw Matt's babies, one leaked on my pants leg, the other drooled down my back. Now Victoria and Nicky."

This was the first time Zac had called Victoria by her name, Libby thought, even if it was in the context of a complaint. Was she beginning to make progress? "Speaking of leaking, I think Nicky's terry suit looks damp. If you want to take Cupcake, I'll change him."

Zac looked at Victoria, who was still chewing on her fist and making little grunts and whimpers that threatened to turn into sobs. He then looked at Nicky, now happy and kicking in his bassinet, a big damp spot in front. He decided to take his chances with him.

His nephew really was kind of cute when he wasn't fussing, Zac decided. He definitely had the determined chin and dark eyes of a true Webster. As Zac removed the wet diaper Nicky cooed and gurgled and kicked his legs in the fresh air. This wasn't so hard, Zac thought.

"Look at him. He's having the time of his life."

"Um, Zac? There's something you ought to know about little boy babies."

"What?"

"It's probably not a good idea to leave his— him exposed while you look for another diaper," she warned.

"Hey, I'm on a roll now. He'll be fine." Zac went into the nursery and came out with a diaper and another stretch terry suit. He knelt down next to the bassinet.

"Hey." Zac stared at the droplets glistening on Nicky's legs and stomach. "How did everything get so wet?"

"Don't say I didn't warn you." Libby smirked at him over Victoria's head.

"I wouldn't dream of it," Zac muttered. He stood, reached down in his trousers, and pulled out the wad of paper towels he'd stuffed in his pants leg. With a sigh he blotted the baby, his knee, then the floor.

When he'd finished, he took a contented and yawning Nicky back to his room and tucked him in the crib. He left the door cracked so he could hear if the baby cried again. Libby, meanwhile, tried putting Victoria back in the bassinet, but the minute she put her down, the baby began fretting.

She looked up and met Zac's gaze. "I'm going to try nursing her. I don't think she's really hungry, but she acts like she could use the comfort." Sitting at one end of the sofa, she tugged up the bottom of her T-shirt. Zac sat at the other end of the sofa, watching intently.

Libby gave him an embarrassed smile, then turned away slightly, but Zac said, "No. Don't. Let me watch. I'd like to watch, Libby."

EIGHT

Her gaze met his and held as she unfastened one cup of her nursing bra. Zac's eyebrows rose. "Neat trick. I didn't notice they did that before, or I might not have bothered with the back fastener."

A half-smile curved his lips as he watched Libby lower her flustered gaze to the eagerly rooting baby. Zac saw her place her fingers on her breast, positioning it just right. She looked up again as Victoria fastened greedily on her nipple. Zac looked from her face to the suckling baby and back, noting the warmth that glowed from her midnight-blue eyes.

He couldn't look away from the scene in front of him—a loving maternal, yet strangely erotic scene. He had a sudden vision of Libby leaning back into his chest, his arms around her, while he held her breast for the baby.

"What does that feel like to you?" he asked softly.

"It—I don't know—it feels good." She stopped for a moment, as if searching for the words. "It makes me feel . . . warm and . . . connected." She sighed. "It's hard to explain."

"It doesn't hurt? I mean, she sucks so hard."

"I was very tender and sore in the beginning, but I got used to it after a week or two, and now it doesn't hurt at all."

Zac watched until he saw Victoria's eyes close and her suckling become less ferocious, less regular, more intermittent. Libby traced the tip of a finger down the side of her baby's face with so much love in her eyes, it almost hurt to see it.

Suddenly Zac thought he understood what Libby had tried to tell him before about setting an example. If he had someone who needed and depended on him the way Victoria needed and depended on Libby, he, too, would do whatever he had to for that person.

Maybe she was right that she and Zac were too different, that each needed something the other couldn't provide. He wanted a warm, passionate, willing, and *temporary* lover. Libby wanted, needed, deserved permanence. Okay, so maybe she was half right. He knew that she was warm and passionate and he wanted her with an ache that went beyond physical. No doubt about it. She was right for him. Perfect.

Maybe it was only that he was wrong for her.

By the time Victoria had gone to sleep, the movie was almost over. Zac and Libby sat in silence staring at the television. Zac couldn't have described what they were watching, not even if he'd been offered a thousand dollars.

Libby also seemed to be having trouble concentrating. She picked at the nail polish on her thumb, she twirled her hair, she twisted her birthstone ring around and around her finger. Zac, watching her in fascination, wondered where her serenity had gone. He'd never before seen her without it.

His own head felt like a busy intersection in five o'clock traffic. Thoughts, ideas, memories, all rushed by each other stopping only momentarily. He pictured Meggy, Pamela's daughter. He'd gone to Pam's for dinner, but the evening had been a disaster. Meggy had whined and fretted and finally kicked Zac in the leg and shouted that she hated him before running to her room in tears.

There was a picture of Matt and Alice's redhaired cherubs who'd screamed as soon as they'd been placed in their uncle Zac's arms. And a picture of Nicky as he'd been earlier this evening, wailing inconsolably.

He saw himself at twenty-one, vowing he'd own his own business by the time he was twenty-five. And he saw himself at twenty-five, vowing he'd be Fortune 500 before ten years had gone by, no matter how much work it took, or how much he had to give up.

And he saw Libby. Libby, with dainty pink toenails, her hair in a shiny curtain down her back, her dark eyes flashing silver blue as she argued a point, and that all-encompassing smile that wrapped around a man's heart. And Libby, the way she'd been just a little while ago, with her lips red and swollen from his kisses, her full breasts bared to his gaze—the most beautiful woman he'd ever seen.

But there was also Libby covered with perspiration and holding her arms out for her newborn infant, and Libby's face glowing with adoration as she cuddled her baby in her arms. And no matter what he felt, or how close they were getting, the baby was—and always would be—there.

As soon as the movie ended, Libby stood. "Hannah should be home anytime now. I'd better get Cupcake home and tucked in her own bed."

"If you wait until Hannah gets here, I'll·see you home."

"I have my car," Libby said gently.

"Oh. That's right. Make sure you drive carefully."

"I always do. I have precious cargo." Libby picked up Victoria, then leaned down for the huge diaper bag she always carried.

"Here, let me get that for you." Zac grabbed the diaper bag and hoisted it over his shoulder. He walked her out to her car and tossed the bag into the backseat while she fastened the baby in the car seat.

She looked up from the baby with a shy smile. "Thanks for—thanks for—"

"Asking you over to save my skin? Not to mention my eardrums. Thank *you* for coming to my rescue." He gave a crooked grin. "I guess sometimes the knights in shining armor are ladies." He ran the back of his hand down her cheek. "Good night, Libby."

Why had it sounded as if he were saying good-bye? Libby wondered as she drove home. Was it the resignation in his eyes, or the finality in his voice? She wasn't sure. She just knew something had changed as he had sat there and watched her nurse Victoria. Every time she'd peeked at him, she'd seen his brows crease as if he were wrestling with a heavy thought. And, finally, as the evening wore on, she'd sensed a subtle but definite withdrawal on his part.

So what had changed? He'd blithely overridden all her objections to their relationship. Had he come up with one he couldn't overcome? If so, what was it? They'd almost made love, for Pete's sake! She'd been nearly mindless with passion in his arms and she thought he'd felt the same. So why had he suddenly turned cold? Was it the sound of Victoria's crying that had done it?

It was after midnight, and she was tired, so maybe her intuition was skewed. She hated to think that their relationship might end so soon—she had a feeling she'd regret it the rest of her life. Yet she was afraid that if things didn't end now, she might regret it even more later.

One A.M. Zac had an eight o'clock meeting Saturday morning with a new distributor, and he couldn't sleep. He paced the floor for a while, then flopped on the couch and stared at the fish. For some reason, it suddenly seemed silly to have fish that matched his living room. Why had he ever agreed to it?

And another thing. It was too quiet. He'd been surrounded all evening by babies crying, the television blaring, and Libby's pleasant chatter. Now the silence that should have been so welcome was getting on his nerves. He turned on the radio, switching the dial from his usual favorite classical station to the heavy throbbing beat of hard rock.

That was better. Maybe all this noise would keep him from thinking. He was afraid that if he thought too much, he might just damn the torpedoes and go after Libby full throttle. But he'd planned his life too long and hard to let anything get in the way now. He was going places. He'd decided that years earlier. And if he was ever going to settle down, it would be after his ten-year plan had been met. Even then—if then—there wouldn't be any kids. His brothers had done their bit to keep the Webster name going, so that let him off the hook.

And while he wanted Libby with a passion that ate at him, he didn't want anything that smacked of permanence, and Libby would settle for nothing less. He'd finally seen that. So he'd drop it. The hunger that burned through him couldn't last forever. Could it? He'd get over it. Someday.

And to help keep his mind off Libby, maybe he'd ask out that curvy blonde he'd met at the racquetball club. He was sure she didn't have anything more permanent in mind than a date for the following weekend.

Out of fairness to Libby, though, maybe he ought to talk to her about it. It was the least he could do. A nice candlelit dinner and good food went a long way to easing hurt feelings. Not that she'd be too upset, he thought. She'd been adamant all along that they wanted different things. Besides, it would be good to see her one last time.

He called Libby Monday morning and asked her out for Friday night. They talked for only a few minutes, since Zac was between meetings, but for some reason the conversation left him feeling good. He whistled as he headed down the hall.

Zac usually enjoyed business meetings. He loved the challenge and stimulation of new ideas and fresh blood. Today, however, his mind kept wandering.

Thoughts of Libby cropped up distracting him at odd moments. The sound of laughter out in the hallway made him think of Libby's laugh. No one had her laugh—musical, infectious, incredibly sexy. A colleague snapped the lid on a shiny black briefcase . . . and Zac thought of Libby's glossy dark hair streaming over her shoulders.

When his secretary handed him a phone message on a pink notepad he thought of the shell-pink polish on Libby's dainty toes.

He was beginning to break out in a sweat. Holding up an impatient hand he suggested: "Why don't we take a five-minute breather?" Without waiting for agreement he left the room and stalked down the hall to the front door. It was a cool, drizzly day, but Zac went outside anyway.

He wished he'd taken up smoking. Maybe a long drag on a menthol cigarette would steady his thinking, but he doubted it. In his younger days he'd have slammed his fist against the wall. Of course, he would probably have broken his hand, since the walls were solid brick. But when he was a kid, he was more concerned with macho posturings and less concerned with getting to the root of the problem. And the problem was Libby. Dammit! Why wouldn't the woman stay out of his head?

He was going to have to solve this problem and solve it fast. Friday night he was either going to tell her they couldn't see each other, or he was going to take her to bed and love her senseless.

All week long, Libby half expected Zac to call with some weak excuse for not going out Friday night. Though she wasn't sure why, her gut instinct told her to watch out for the Dear Jill call. Every time the phone rang, her heart pounded and she had to force herself to answer it. It was never Zac.

She wanted to call him—she missed talking to him, seeing him, feeling his strength surround her—but she sensed that things between them had changed.

Hannah seemed to confirm this on Wednesday afternoon when they took the babies to the park and ate lunch in the shade of the old maple trees that lined the walk. The first words out of Hannah's mouth were "What in the world did you do to Zac?"

Libby who had bent down to take Victoria out of the baby carrier, paused, then straightened. "What do you mean? I didn't do anything to Zac."

"He sure has been subdued the past few days. He probably said all of two words to me when I got back Friday night; he said maybe three words when he came over for Sunday dinner. I figured you either knocked him upside the head or kissed him silent."

Libby took the baby out of the carrier and placed her on a blanket spread on the grass. "Hannah, I have no earthly idea what goes on in that man's head. Everything was fine Friday night. We talked, watched television, and everything was fine. Next thing I know, he's staring across the room in a blue funk. I was hoping you could tell me."

Hannah opened the lid on the box of chicken she'd picked up on the way to the park. "I wish I could help you. But if it's any consolation, I think you've got him tied in knots."

"I don't think it's me," Libby said morosely. "I think it's the baby. You know, the other night I saw a glimmer of how good he could be with kids if he let down his guard. He and Nicky actually had a friendly truce going there for a while. Next thing I know, Nicky's asleep and Zac's looking at Victoria as if she had two heads and six eyes."

"Well," Hannah said around a mouthful of fried chicken, "he's got to get used to babies sooner or later. I mean, he's got two nieces and a nephew all under two."

"But he doesn't see the twins all that often, does he?"

"He gets up to New York two or three times a year and Matt and Alice come down here every so often. And when they do, they usually stay with Zac."

"Why? Don't you have more room?"

Hannah's face shadowed. "Things are a bit strained between Matt and me. He thinks I should make more of an effort to get in touch with Ben. He and Ben are very close."

"But you told Ben you were pregnant."

"I sent him a letter when I first found out. I'd been confined to bed for a few weeks because of some bleeding, and I begged Ben to come home. He never even answered the letter. The next and last time I had any contact with him was when I sent him the divorce papers. Last time anybody heard from him was a letter he sent to Matt, saying he was taking a special consulting assignment in the Middle East and would be out of touch for a while. But I've pretty much resigned myself to the fact that he's not coming back. Nicky and I will have to make our own life."

She sighed. "Let's talk about something less depressing. Like when you're seeing Zac again."

"Friday night." Libby reached for one of the small containers of potato salad.

Hannah took another bite of chicken and chewed thoughtfully. "If I'm being too nosy, just say so. How do you feel about my erstwhile brother-in-law?"

"He makes me feel like I've got a bad case of prickly heat."

Hannah laughed. "I thought so. He's quite a guy, isn't he?"

"Yeah. Quite a guy. Quite gorgeous, quite bright, quite stubborn and pigheaded and arrogant and—"

"I get the picture. Don't give up too easy, Libby. He might be a tough nut to crack, but he's worth the trouble. And, if it means anything to you, I think you're good for him." She picked up another piece of chicken. "And I think you give him prickly heat too."

Deb called first thing Friday morning. "Libby? I can't sit for you tonight."

"Why? Is something wrong?"

"Yeah, I'm dying." She stopped for a moment, sneezed twice, then continued. "Or else I'm already dead and don't know it yet." She sneezed again.

"You sound terrible."

"The doctor says it's just an allergy, but what does he know? It feels like pneumonia to me. I hope this doesn't cause a problem for you."

"Oh, no. No, everything will be fine. I'm sure I can get Hannah." Libby promised to call Deb later to check on her, then called Hannah.

"Gee, I'm sorry, Libby," Hannah said apologetically, "but I'm just on the way out the door. I'm driving to Jersey to spend the weekend with my parents."

Libby thanked her and stared at the phone in dismay. She didn't mind cooking dinner for Zac at her house, but that was probably all it would take to scare him off completely. She didn't know what else to do, though, so she called Zac's office.

His secretary answered the phone, and Libby paused for a moment at the soft, sultry voice she heard. That was a bedroom voice if she'd ever heard one. She quickly stifled the jealousy that stabbed through her and asked to speak to Zac.

"He's in a meeting," the sexy voice said. "May I take a message?"

"Would you please ask him to call Libby Austin when he gets a chance? He has my number." She carefully replaced the receiver and bit her lip. So what did she do now? Did she sit and wait for him to call, or did she run to the grocery store in case he chose to come to dinner? She decided not to take any chances and went to the store.

The telephone was ringing as soon as she opened the door, a bag of groceries balanced precariously in one arm, the baby in the other. She plopped the bag on the counter, where it promptly fell, scattering groceries everywhere and startling Victoria so that she let out a wail. "Hello?"

"This is Zac."

Right, Libby thought, like it was really necessary for him to identify himself when the first word out of his mouth caused an army of goose bumps to march up her spine. "Hello, Zac." She raised her voice over the baby's cries. "My sitter fell through for tonight. I thought we could eat dinner here if you want."

There was a long pause on the other end of the line, then Zac finally said, "Maybe it wouldn't be such a good idea. It sounds like the baby isn't doing so well today."

Libby propped the baby on her shoulder and began a rhythmic patting on her back. "She's fine, really. She's just a bit cranky from missing her nap. I have all the ingredients for fettuccine Alfredo," she said, knowing it was one of his favorite dishes.

"Fettuccine Alfredo? Well, if you're sure the baby is all right . . . what time?"

"Seven? That was the time we originally planned to go out."

"I'll see you at seven, then. Should I bring a bottle of wine?"

"I'm abstaining while I'm still nursing. But feel free to bring a bottle if you'd like. I don't need anything else. I have a loaf of Italian bread from the deli and I'll toss a salad."

"If you won't drink, then I won't. But I insist on bringing something," Zac said with a tone of finality. "I'll stop by Guido's and pick up some spumoni."

"That sounds wonderful. See you at seven." Libby's hand lingered on the phone long after she'd hung up the receiver. This wasn't a good idea, she knew, but she was fascinated by Zac, intrigued by him, mesmerized by him. And in love with him.

The knowledge came as no big surprise to her. It was just something she knew about herself. She had black hair, blue eyes, a baby, a dog, and an overwhelming love for one Zachary Webster.

Great. Just what she needed. Not only was he *not* in love with her, but she had a strong feeling that he was searching for a tactful way to get out of the whole situation.

She sighed and sat down to rock Victoria for a few minutes before starting on preliminary preparations for dinner. With a baby, things didn't always go as planned, so she figured she'd better get as much done ahead of time as possible.

Nevertheless, by the time she'd washed and dried her hair, fed and walked the dog, fed Victoria and played with her for a little while, she had only fifteen or twenty minutes left to get dressed. That would have been just enough time if only Zac had not arrived fifteen minutes early.

Libby, wearing only a towel, peered around the door and gave Zac an embarrassed smile. "Um, hi. You're early."

He glanced at his watch. "I guess I am." He wasn't about to tell her it was because he couldn't wait to get there. He might never see her again after tonight, and this one last evening with her mattered to him. "Can I come in, or would you rather have me wait out here until seven? I'm not sure how the spumoni will hold up, though." He grinned at her, relishing the rare flustered look on her face and enjoying the fact that he had been the one to put it there.

"I'm not exactly dressed, but—" She broke off as Victoria began to fret. Clutching her towel, Libby opened the door a little wider. "I guess you'd better come in."

As Zac stepped into the living room, she immediately dashed to the bedroom, affording him only a glimpse of her impossibly long, slender legs and creamy, bare shoulders. God, he was hungry—and it had nothing to do with fettuccine Alfredo. Just then a small sound reminded him he wasn't alone, and he gave a nervous glance toward the baby propped up in a baby seat. "I guess it's just you and me, kid, huh?"

Victoria was wearing a frilly pink dress. A matching pink bow was fastened to her one curl of fine dark hair. She stared up at him with solemn blue eyes, then kicked out one tiny bare foot in a tentative overture. When that didn't work, she kicked out both feet.

Zac squatted down in front of the baby. "Uh, hi."

She waved her arms at him, but didn't cry, so he felt braver. "How's it going?"

Victoria waved her arms again, still staring at him. He held out his finger and the baby immediately grasped it. Zac said, "I need to spend some quiet time with your mom tonight. So would you please think about going to sleep early? You get to have her every day. I just want to borrow her for a while this evening. If you're really good, then I'll bring you—well, I don't guess you can handle a lollipop yet—so I'll bring you some strained peaches or something. Okay?" He gave a little shake to her tiny hand. "Deal?"

NINE

For a moment Zac marveled at how tightly the baby held on to his finger, as if it were something important she didn't want to let go. She really was a cute little thing—when she wasn't crying, that is.

As for Libby, Zac still wasn't sure whether he was going to try to end this relationship amicably or continue it passionately. Maybe they'd get the chance to explore their options tonight without interruptions.

The dog began whining outside the back door. Remembering what Libby said the night he came to dinner about the dog disturbing the neighbors, he went to let him in. Bracing himself, he opened the kitchen door. The dog bounded in, wagging and yipping with joy, and immediately jumped on

Zac. He tried to keep his face out of firing range of that two-foot-long tongue.

Victoria apparently didn't like being alone, because her disgruntled kicks and fretful whimpers now degenerated into screams. Zac went over to her and eyed her uncertainly. Lord, she put her whole body into it, that was for sure. Her face turned red, her little fists clenched, her feet kicked out angrily. He could only admire her wholehearted determination.

Libby poked her head out of the bedroom. "Zac, would you mind picking her up and just walking her a minute? She's tired, but she's fighting it. She'll settle down soon, and I'll only be a few more minutes. Thanks." She shut the bedroom door again.

Pick her up? She had to be kidding. Didn't Libby know by now the effect that Zac had on babies? With a grimace he lifted the baby into his arms, this time holding her the way Libby had showed him the other night. He held his breath, waiting for the real wails to begin. Instead, the fussing calmed down to a little whimpers. Then, when Zac offered her the pacifier that she'd been lying on in the baby seat, the crying stopped altogether.

Victoria looked up at him, her tiny mouth working the pacifier furiously. Zac watched as her long, dark lashes—so like her mother's—fluttered once, twice, then closed. He continued to look down at her. Her skin was so soft—he didn't think he'd ever felt anything as soft. And she was so tiny. Was it his imagination, or did she look a lot like Libby? She did. She had the same curve to her cheek, the same dark blue eyes, even the same stubborn chin. And her one curl of hair was the same rich dark color.

"Thanks."

Zac turned around at the softly spoken words, then stared, his mouth suddenly dry. She wore a short red skirt with a matching short top, both made of soft cotton T-shirt fabric that outlined the lush curves beneath. But that wasn't the only thing that made his heart pound and his palms begin to sweat.

It was the gold thong sandals she wore on her sexy bare feet that revealed the bright red polish on each and every toenail. Zac wasn't sure, but he thought he groaned.

"Why don't you put Cupcake in her crib?" Libby asked, and led the way down the hall: He gently lay Victoria down on her tummy in her crib. Libby tucked a soft pink and green flannel sheet over the baby's bare legs and turned out the light. "Thanks for getting her to sleep for me. She settled right down once you picked her up."

Zac shook his head ruefully and followed her into the kitchen.

Dinner went well. At least Zac thought so. He didn't remember a thing he'd eaten. He couldn't keep his attention on his food—or off her long, long legs and delectable toes. But it wasn't just that.

Every word she said, every gesture she made, was engraved on his mind. If he lived to be a hundred and ten, he didn't think he'd forget the way her hair cascaded down her back or the way her eyes lightened and sparkled when she laughed or the way she pursed her lips when she was thinking. Here he'd thought the evening would be so simple. Just have a nice little heart-to-heart and be on his merry way. Or spend one, count 'em, one memorable night in her bed—and *then* be on his merry way.

He didn't think it was so simple now. He realized he couldn't tell her he didn't want to see her anymore because he *did* want to see her again. And again and again. And he had a sick feeling in his gut that one night in her bed wouldn't be enough. Not nearly enough.

"Is everything okay?"

Zac blinked his eyes and looked down at his plate. Fettuccine Alfredo. Most of it was gone, so he assumed he'd eaten it. "Everything's fine. The fettuccine is delicious." It could have been wood shavings topped with vinegar and he doubted he would have known the difference. He noticed that it was hot in here, though. It had started out as a mild summer day, but the temperature seemed to have climbed steadily since he'd gotten there—or at least since she'd walked out in that killer red outfit.

This was a big, big mistake. He should have left well enough alone. If he had any sense, he'd thank her for dinner and take his leave. If he had any sense of self-preservation, he'd run for the hills. It was much too dangerous to stay. Unfortunately, he'd never been deterred by a little danger. As a matter of fact, he'd always been intrigued by it.

He usually played it safe, though he had flirted with skydiving lessons a few years ago and had even been toying with the idea of bungee jumping. The lure and promise of her danger was too seductive to resist.

"Do you want dessert now or later?"

"Later." He watched her fiddle with her silverware. He had something different in mind for dessert.

"What are you staring at?" she asked.

"You." A rueful half-smile curved his lips. No

doubt about it, when he decided to give in, he gave in with wholehearted enthusiasm.

"Why?"

"I'm trying to decide what I want to do first. Do I want to kiss you till your eyes cross, or do I want to peel off that sexy top of yours and fill my hands with your breasts? Or do I want to kiss the backs of your knees until they buckle? What do you think?"

She could perfectly envision him doing all of those things he'd mentioned. She'd dreamed about them often enough, but his words came as a surprise considering the way he'd been the last time they parted. Unsure how to react, she practically jumped up off her chair, saying, "I have to do the dishes, and I think you should go into the living room and wait."

"I'll help."

Please, don't. "No! I mean, it's not necessary. It won't take long."

"I'll help," Zac repeated as he stood and carried his plate to the sink, turned on the water, and rinsed it off. "You wash, I'll dry."

"Zac, I can manage," Libby said, but didn't think it would do any good. Zac had that steely, determined glint in his eye that said he wanted to hang around and make her nervous. He was doing a top-notch job of it too. Heavens, but the man confused her!

As she filled the sink with water, Zac came up behind her with an apron and put it around her waist. He managed to brush his fingers down the sides of her hips as he did so, but when she turned a suspicious glance on him, he flashed an absolutely cherubic smile and tied the sash in back. She glared at him and picked up a plate.

"You missed a spot," Zac said as he reached across in front of her to point, managing to brush his hand across her breasts as he did so.

"I haven't washed it yet," she muttered, and picked up the sponge. She angled her body away so he wouldn't see the automatic response of her breasts to his touch.

"Oops! Sorry." He didn't sound at all apologetic.

"Zac, please go in the other room." She wanted to cringe at the desperate sound of her voice. But she really needed a few minutes, or she was going to blurt out how she felt. Her feelings were still new and overwhelming, and she was already dangerously close to telling him. Only she was afraid he didn't want to hear it and it might be the impetus that propelled him right out the door. And she didn't want him to go.

"I'm going to help," Zac said.

"Help me right out of my mind, you mean."

"I'd rather help you out of your clothes." He tugged her back against him so he could nuzzle aside her hair and kiss the nape of her neck, then his fingers unerringly found and brushed across her pouting nipples. She twisted in his hands and faced him, the wet sponge hitting him square in the chest.

"Yow!" He jumped back a step. "What was that for?"

She smiled grimly. "Retribution."

"Oh. Well, turnabout is fair play, they say." He took the sponge, dipped it in the warm soapy water, and held it up.

Libby retreated a step. "You wouldn't dare."

Zac grinned. "You don't think so?"

She shook her head uncertainly.

"You're right," he said, dropping the sponge into the sink. "I can think of forms of retribution I like better."

"Like what?" She eyed him with suspicion.

"I'll think about it and let you know." He grabbed the bottom of his damp shirt and pulled it over his head, then tossed it over the back of a chair.

Her eyes widened. Heavens to Betsy, he was gorgeous—broad and golden tan, with little whorls of dark hair just on the upper portion of his chest.

Libby swallowed hard, her eyes glued to his body. The other night, when she had touched him, she hadn't really looked at him. She'd been too engrossed in the feelings he was arousing in her. But now she let her hungry gaze wander freely. She'd never before thought a man could be beautiful. But that was the only word that could describe him.

She wondered briefly, foggily, how a desk jockey kept such a nice tan, then decided she didn't care. She just cared that he looked wonderful—strong, solid, secure. And here.

"When you look at me like that, you make me want to touch you. More than anything else in the world, I want to touch you." His voice vibrated with his need.

Their gazes locked, and Libby asked herself if this was wise. Maybe not, but she wanted him, trusted him. Loved him. She'd begun to realize that he couldn't, or wouldn't give her the security she needed, but did she want to go through life never knowing what it would have been like to have been loved by him, however briefly?

She took a step toward him, her need transparent. But he didn't touch her right away; instead, he looked long and hard at her. "Think about it, Libby. Because, God help me, if I start, I'm not going to stop this time—unless the house caves in." He gave a ghost of a smile. "And maybe not then."

God, she was scared. This was going to change her life. But then, just *knowing* him had already done that. She was mesmerized by the sudden flames that danced to life in his eyes—flames that promised to set her on fire with the heat of their passion. "I don't want you to stop." Was that breathless whisper really her voice?

Zac reached out a hand to her, then dropped it to his side, his fist clenched. "If you need to go check on the baby, go now. I might not be able to let you go later."

Obediently, Libby turned and went to Victoria's room, making sure the infant was dry and sleeping peacefully. She stopped by the bathroom to run a brush through her hair, then paused for a moment, staring at her reflection in the mirror. Her eyes glistened with anticipation and her lips curved in a tremulous smile. Her face was so clearly that of a woman in love, she was amazed Zac hadn't seen it.

A frisson of apprehension ran down her spine. Bobby had been the only man she'd ever been with, and she had always assumed that the reason she hadn't enjoyed sex more was that he'd been an impatient, often selfish lover. But suppose she hadn't enjoyed it because she was no good at it?

Certainly Bobby had never taken the time to introduce her to any of the finer points of love-making.

Suppose Zac found her sadly lacking and hopelessly inexperienced? Her jaw firmed. What she didn't have in finesse she'd just have to make up for with love and enthusiasm. And she had plenty of that. Smoothing an errant strand of hair back off her face, she went into the living room.

Zac was standing next to the picture window, peering out between the trailing stems of the huge ivy that flourished there. Libby watched him for a moment, uncertain what to do next.

He looked over at her, smiled, and held out his hand. "Come here, baby." He clasped her hand in his and turned back to look out the window. "Look."

Libby tore her gaze from him long enough to see the fading colors of what had to have been a spectacular sunset. The orange and rose streaks were giving way to deeper blues and purples which would soon disappear, swallowed up by the black velvet sky. "It's beautiful."

"Come outside and watch it with me." Still holding her hand, he tugged her outside and pulled her down to sit next to him on the top step of the front porch.

Libby was thoroughly confused. Wasn't he

going to make love to her? "Zac? I thought you . . . we . . ." She stopped. How could she possibly ask him if he had changed his mind?

"We have all the time in the world," he murmured, and put his arm around her, drawing her close. "But right now I need to slow it down some. You make me feel too much like a teenager with his first girl, and I want our first time to be long and slow and wonderful for you."

Would he never cease to amaze her? She was touched by his concern for her as they sat watching the sky slowly darken, though she had no doubt that it would be wonderful with him no matter what, and her pulse quickened and her breath caught at the thought of a long, slow night with him.

Zac kept his arm around her, the fingers of his hand threading through her hair. As they watched the last faint purple streaks disappear, Libby became increasingly aware of him, hearing his measured breathing, feeling the beating of his heart as if it were her own, feeling her skin become more and more sensitized to his every move. His hand left her hair and traced slow, sensuous circles on the back of her neck, making Libby wonder how Zac would react if she melted into a boneless puddle on the porch step.

He finally stood, held out a hand to help her to her feet, and whispered, "Now, Libby."

Wordlessly, she nodded and led him to her bedroom. She sat on the edge of the bed and reached down to unbuckle one of the gold sandals. "Not yet." He stopped her, tugging her to her feet and running his hands down her arms. "You're so beautiful, Libby. Did you know, when I first saw you, I thought you looked like a Madonna—so cool and serene."

"A Madonna?"

He nodded. "But when I saw your eyes, that's when I knew there was a warm, passionate woman underneath." He held her gaze with his own as he ran his hands just beneath the bottom of the short top, then lifted it over her head and tossed it aside.

"I wanted you even then." He pulled the elastic-waist skirt down over her hips and let it slither to her feet.

"But the first time I kissed you, and we both went up in smoke, that's when I knew we were going to make love." He stopped talking as his gaze fell on her red lace bra and matching panties. "Oh, God," he breathed. "I may not survive this night. Did you know red's my favorite color?"

"I know."

He traced a finger around the lacy edge of her bra, then brought long strands of hair around to fall over her breasts. He arranged them like a silk curtain, letting only glimpses of the red lace show through. "This isn't any nursing bra, either, is it?" He reached around her to unfasten it. When the clasp popped free, he slid the straps down her arms and tossed the lace scrap aside. His breath rasped as he reached out and gently brushed her hair aside, baring her to his gaze. He laid a palm flat above her breast. "I can feel your heart beating," he murmured. "It's like a part of me."

He cupped a breast in each hand, fascinated with the warm, heavy weight, then ran a thumb lightly over each pebbled pink tip, teasing them to aching rosiness. Libby gasped as if the feeling was almost too intense to bear.

Her nipples leaked a little, but Zac just massaged the droplets into her breasts. "Watch," he whispered, his voice barely audible. "Watch my hands touch you."

Libby looked down, hypnotized by the sight of his large hands touching her so intimately. She noticed that his hands were trembling slightly, and she felt an answering shiver begin deep inside her.

She reached out her hands, now trembling to match his, and ran them over his chest. "Watch me touch you," she said as she repeated his motion and ran her thumbs over his nipples, satisfied at their pucker.

When he drew his thumbs in slow, tantalizing circles around the tight buds of her nipples, she did the same to him, causing him to draw in a deep, shuddering breath. He allowed his hands to slip down to her waist, and she let her hands do the same, pausing in breathless wonder.

As he hooked his fingers in the lacy waistband of her panties, Libby rapidly unbuckled his belt and unfastened his zipper. When Zac began to slide her panties down an inch at a time, she did the same with his trousers.

He put his hands on hers and stilled them. "Please, baby," he pleaded hoarsely, "let me do this my way. This first time. The next time will be all yours, but if you touch me anymore, I'll go off like a Fourth of July firecracker."

"I don't care if it's quick the first time."

He drew her hand to his lips and kissed the back of it. "But I care. I want to spend all night loving you."

He urged her down on the bed, then sat on the edge next to her feet. Lifting her left foot into his lap, he slowly unfastened the buckle on the sandal and slid the shoe off, dropping it onto the floor. He felt himself grow harder and hotter as he massaged every last inch of her foot, from her toe to her heel and back. His fingers caressed a path from her ankles over the top of her foot and around to the instep.

Libby drew in her breath and curled her toes. Only then did he turn his attention to the other foot. When her eyes closed as if to savor the sensation, he began moving his wicked fingers to her ankle, then her calf, then her knee, then her thigh. She moaned, and he finally moved his hands up over her hips and slid her panties the rest of the way off.

Zac sat next to her for a long time, looking at her, almost afraid to touch. Slow and easy, he told himself over and over, as if saying it would somehow make it happen. But his self-control already hung in tatters.

He'd never imagined how beautiful she'd be with her black satin hair tangled over the pillows. Her skin was smooth cream, her body perfectly proportioned. Her full breasts with their rosy tips topped a narrow waist, and her stomach was smooth and flat with only a few faint silver lines marking it. He traced one with the very tip of his finger.

Her eyes opened. "Stretch marks," she said, her voice muffled, and she laid her hand flat on her stomach as if to hide them.

"Marks of courage and strength." He pulled her hand away and traced another mark with his finger, then bent suddenly, and followed behind with his tongue. Her whimpers of pleasure shot through him like hot arrows, adding to the need that churned inside him.

It was a basic need, a primitive need, a need to claim and conquer. And it was a need he'd never before had. Before, there had been a desire only for momentary pleasure; now there was a need for more. He couldn't put words to it. He just knew he had to make his feelings known to her—feelings so deep and rich that he couldn't name them. But somehow, maybe, she'd understand.

With a communication that transcended words, he showed his feelings with a lover's touch—touching, caressing, kissing. Every time she moaned or gasped with pleasure, it served to spur him on. Like a thirsty man at a pool of cool water, he drank in her sweetness, letting it fill him up until it spilled over.

There wasn't an inch of her that he didn't taste—from the base of her throat to the curve of her waist to the backs of her knees to her candy-apple-red toenails. And when he finally tasted the already damp petals of her womanhood, she tangled her fingers in his hair and arched her hips as the tremors of ecstasy shook her body. He felt each spasm as acutely as if she were connected to him.

"Please, Zac. Please. Now." She urged his body up to lay atop hers.

"Now," he agreed with a groan. He bent over the side of the bed and fumbled in his trouser pocket for a moment, then turned back into her eagerly waiting arms. With his body poised above hers, he whispered, "Look at me, baby. I want to see your eyes when you take me inside you." Their gazes locked, he slid into the hot, sweet pleasure that awaited him.

As their bodies moved together, he was rocked to his very soul at the intensity of the feelings that swept through him—feelings that were by turns shaky, sure, gentle, savage, generous, greedy. With the last shreds of his self-control, he held on until he felt more tremors shake her body. Then he plunged deep and buried his face in her neck.

"Oh, God, Libby," he groaned over and over as the lightning bolts of fulfillment shot through him. And as they clung together in the midst of spiraling fireworks, he found words welling up from inside—words he didn't know had been lying in wait. "I love you, baby. I love you."

Later, as they lay curled together, drowsy and sated, he wasn't sure whether he'd actually said the words out loud. But, strangely enough, they didn't scare him. At least, not like the idea of falling in love had a year or two ago. Love didn't automatically have to mean marriage—not these days.

Even though marriage wasn't in his plans for the next few years, he could certainly work in a relationship. He'd have to. Now that he knew what making love with her was like, he intended to make time for it. A whole lot of time. He conveniently chose to ignore thoughts of the baby sleeping in the other room. Of course, Libby wanted a permanent relationship, but after last night, maybe she'd be content to just share his bed. It was all he had to give her.

He drew Libby closer and nuzzled the top of her head, breathing in that sweet honeysuckle and baby talc fragrance that clung to her. "You okay?" He toyed with her hair, spreading it over the pillow.

"Better than okay," Libby murmured against the warm, damp skin of his chest. "More like great. Wonderful, even. How about you?"

Zac sighed, a deep, sated sigh of contentment, and his voice was husky with promise when he said, "If I had known just how wonderful it was going to be, I'd have jumped your bones a long time ago."

Libby smiled and curled her fingers through the hair on his chest. "Not if I jumped yours first." She found and lazily circled one tight male nipple. She could feel the sudden acceleration in his heartbeat beneath her cheek.

"Ahem." Zac cleared his throat. "Speaking of jumping bones . . ."

"Yes?"

"You're welcome to jump mine now, if you like. And I devoutly wish you would."

"Now?" Libby raised her head to look at him. "You mean like right now? You're not going to turn over and go to sleep?"

"Of course not! That would be a tragic waste of time, what with you in my arms and all. Besides"—he turned to the side so she could feel his renewed desire—"I did say next time would be all yours, didn't I?"

One more reason to damn Bobby, Libby thought. So some men didn't automatically roll over and doze, like Bobby said they did. Or was Zac the exception? She felt his rapidly growing erection against her thigh. If he was an exception, he was certainly an exceptional exception.

She smiled to herself, her hands beginning a wonderful voyage of exploration. Now it was her turn to drive him as crazy with need as he had her. She smoothed the palms of her hands over his chest and he moaned deep in his throat. She sucked each flat brown nipple and his breath caught. She slid one seeking hand down over his stomach to his throbbing arousal and he gulped, then rolled over, pinning her beneath him.

Her eyes shone up at him. "I don't know how good I am at this, Zac, but—"

"Baby, if you were any better at this, it'd kill me."

He lowered his lips to hers. "I love kissing you," he said against her mouth. "I could kiss you for hours and hours." He cupped her breast in his hand. "And I love touching you here. I could do this for hours, but then I wouldn't have time to do this. . . ." He slipped a finger inside her. Just before the waves of passion inundated her completely, a thought hit her. Although he was willing to admit it only when he was in the throes of passion, he did love her. But would love be enough?

TEN

Libby woke before Zac did the next morning. She lay on her side, Zac nestled against her back as close as a second skin. His arm was draped over her, his hand cupping her breast. Libby gently, reluctantly, disengaged herself from his grasp and stretched, smiling to herself at the telltale soreness that spoke of a night in Zac's arms. It was a wonderful soreness, a sensual soreness. He had kept his promise, she thought fancifully, it had been long and slow—at least the first time.

The second time, her time, had been fast and furious. And in the middle of the night, when she'd gotten up to nurse the baby, he'd awakened when she got back in bed and pulled her to him for another hungry exploration.

Her gaze wandered leisurely over his face, seeing the man beneath the pose. Tiny lines beside his eyes said that he laughed often. His jaw still jutted obstinately, even in sleep, and that devilish curve to his lips still remained, warning the world that he'd always be able to give as good as he got. His whiskers were just starting to show, and Libby's eyes widened in humor. Red. His beard was coming in red. No wonder he never showed signs of a five o'clock shadow.

He was definitely a man for a lifetime—one to wake up to every morning. His lips did have that permanent humorous quirk, but also showed a capacity for tenderness. His jaw was stubborn, true, but also ambitious and determined without being obsessive. It was that determination that was going to give her the most trouble, she realized, because he was as determined to stay single as she was to get married. She resolutely pushed away the feeling that this had been a big mistake.

Zac murmured and reached out for her, his hand cupping a breast. The pressure reminded her how sore and swollen she was, and she glanced at the clock. Eight o'clock? She sat bolt upright in bed. Cupcake had never slept this late before. Heart pounding, she scrambled out of bed and dashed into the baby's room, only to find Victoria lying on her back, playing contentedly with her toes.

As soon as the baby saw Libby, she grinned

and let out a gurgle of delight, waving her arms in the air. With a sigh of relief, Libby picked up the baby, cuddling her against her neck. "Thanks a lot, sweetie," she murmured. "Thanks for giving me an almost uninterrupted night. I put it to good use. I promise."

"You did that," a voice agreed from the doorway.

Libby looked up with a smile, and her breath caught in her throat at the sight of Zac outlined in the morning light. His stance was wide, his arms crossed and he looked as magnificently regal, even stark naked, as an approving pasha surveying his harem.

"Good morning," she said shyly.

Zac came over to her and wrapped his arms around her and the baby. "Come back to bed, Libby. I didn't like waking up without you."

"I'm sorry," she murmured against the warm skin of his throat. "I had to go see why Victoria was sleeping so late."

"I bribed her, that's why."

"Bribed her?"

"Last night. I promised her strained peaches or something if she gave us an interrupted night."

"As soon as she's ready to start solid food, I'll be sure to work it in. Right now, though, I think she's ready to nurse." She could feel the baby's inquisitive little mouth making sucking motions against her shoulder.

"Bring her back to bed with you, then. After all"—his voice was laced with humor—"that's about the only place we're both dressed for."

She turned and grabbed a diaper from the dresser and headed back to the bedroom. Zac appreciatively eyed the smooth flesh of her bare buttocks as she preceded him. Libby moved with a natural, unstudied grace and seemed not the least bit self-conscious about her body. He liked that. He really liked a woman who was comfortable with her own body—though he'd met very few who actually were.

Her figure wasn't perfect, at least not by today's standards. Her curves were a little too pronounced for the tight-jeans-and-T-shirt look, but they were the kind of curves that demanded to be explored and claimed. A man could spend the rest of his life exploring them. But the man wouldn't—couldn't—be him.

Zac sat next to her on the bed, and she immediately handed him the baby and the diaper. "What's this for?" He raised an eyebrow.

Libby fluttered her eyelashes. "To change her."

"Change her into what?" he grinned. "I thought you liked her the way she is."

"Cute. Real cute. No, I thought you'd change

her diaper." When Zac started to protest, she held up a hand. "Don't tell me you don't change diapers. You did a perfectly good job changing Nicky's."

"Except when he leaked."

"All babies leak."

Zac sighed good-naturedly. "All right." He unsnapped the baby's terry sleeper.

For someone who hadn't changed that many diapers in his life—and for someone who swore he wasn't good with babies—he was surprisingly competent. He had the baby changed and powdered and tucked into a clean terry suit in a matter of minutes. Libby silently thanked God that Victoria was not only in her usual morning good mood, but that she even seemed to be showing off.

She kicked her feet, smiled, cooed, blew bubbles, and gave a big toothless grin whenever Zac looked at her. He reached out and ran a finger down her petal-soft cheek. The baby turned her head toward his finger and grabbed it, sucking vigorously. Zac turned a puzzled glance to Libby.

She reached over and lifted the baby into her arms. "She's telling you, in a very gentle way, that she's ready for breakfast."

"Let me help."

"I'm afraid there's really nothing you can do—"

Zac leaned against the head of the bed and pulled Libby back against him. "I can do this." He reached around and circled her breast with his hand, positioning the nipple just right for the baby's eagerly sucking mouth. He continued to hold Libby in his hand while the baby nursed.

As he peered over her shoulder at the baby nestled in her arms, he felt a strange warmth inside. He was as turned on as he could get—and he knew Libby could feel his arousal by the way she kept scooting back against it. But it wasn't only that he found it all incredibly erotic, he also found it moving and—what was that word Libby had used?—connected. He felt connected.

The baby was starting to get full—at least that's what Zac guessed by the way she had become less interested in nursing and more interesting in playing. Whenever she'd see Zac peek over Libby's shoulder, Victoria would give a big grin around the rosy nipple still in her mouth. Finally, she let go altogether and began blowing little milky bubbles as she played with her feet.

Zac touched a droplet of milk still clinging to Libby's swollen pink nipple. "What does that taste like, I wonder?" He eased Libby to one side and lowered his head toward her breast.

"Zac." Did Libby know how sexy she sounded

with that breathless pleading in her voice? "I need to burp Cupcake."

"And I need to make love to you. But I suppose I can wait—for a minute or two." He leaned back against the pillows and watched Libby as she put the baby against her shoulder and gently patted her back. Victoria kept peeking at Zac and smiling, and Zac couldn't help but smile back. *God, but she was a cute kid!*

When a few minutes had gone by with no results, Zac leaned forward and touched his nose to the baby's. "Burp," he ordered softly. Victoria grinned, blew bubbles at him, and let out a very satisfying burp. Libby immediately put her in the baby seat and positioned it so Victoria could see the rays of sun filtering through the assorted plants that filled the window. She turned back to Zac with a smile, only to have Wells take a flying leap and land in the middle of the bed.

Zac rolled his eyes. "And what does he want?"

"To go out, I guess."

"I'll go put him in the backyard and"—he looked daggers at the madly wagging dog—"I defy you to bark even once. Is that clear?" The dog wagged twice and ran to the kitchen door. Zac was back in less than a minute, but instead of getting into the bed, he walked to the telephone, lifted the receiver, and shut it in the nightstand drawer.

"You're a man of many talents, Mr. Webster," Libby said admiringly. "You change babies like a pro, get them to burp, order dogs not to bark, and even figure out how to prevent telephone interruptions."

"Wait till you see what else I can do." He sat on the edge of the bed and lifted her left foot in his hand.

"I can hardly wait," she murmured with a moan as he began tracing circles on her big toe— with his tongue.

By mutual consent they missed breakfast. They almost missed lunch too, but their stomachs reminded them. Libby didn't think she'd ever been this happy in her life, though she knew she was only borrowing the happiness for a short while. They giggled like children as they fixed lunch together—Zac even made bologna sandwiches seem sexy, especially when he squeezed a dollop of mustard over the curve of Libby's breast and proceeded to lick it off. This delayed lunch by another half hour and the tomato soup Libby had heated was nearly cold, but they ate it anyway.

Zac went home midafternoon, after arranging

to pick Libby up for dinner at his place that evening. Libby sat on the sofa after he'd gone, cuddling Victoria. No sooner had the door shut than the house seemed to echo with emptiness. She couldn't stand it.

She propped the baby on her shoulder and wandered into the kitchen, but stopped short at the disorder that greeted her—disorder that whispered Zac. The dishes from lunch were stacked in the sink, and there was a smear of mustard on the countertop—mustard from Zac's sexy play. She shook her head. She'd deal with this later.

She went into the bedroom to get the baby chair, but here the emptiness didn't just echo, it yelled, it screamed at her. The rumpled sheets, the scraps of red lace scattered on the floor all shouted Zac's name.

She cuddled the baby closer. Had this been a mistake? A woman who wanted, needed, a husband, and a man who didn't want to need anyone—it was impossible. Based on how empty her cozy little house felt after just one night with him, she began to see the magnitude of her mistake. She had set herself up for the heartache of a lifetime.

Zac showered and changed as soon as he got in the door, then turned on the television. He listened to the baseball game with half a mind while he restlessly prowled his apartment. He was ready to go over to Libby's right then and get her, but he'd said he'd pick her up at six. Three more hours.

He looked around his living room, not quite satisfied for some reason. He rearranged the silk plants on his mantel, opened the sheer curtains to let in more light, even moved all the magazines from the coffee table. But something still didn't seem right. He took off his shoes and socks and left them piled in front of the sofa as he paced. Suddenly he stopped and looked at them. For some odd reason, the clutter made it look better. It's a shame there wasn't more color, though.

A sudden flash of inspiration made Zac put his socks and shoes back on, grab his car keys, and dash out. He was back in less than an hour with a vase filled with a huge bouquet of flowers—blue, yellow, purple, red. Lots of red. He set that on the coffee table and nodded in satisfaction. Libby would love it.

He showed up at her house at five-thirty. "You're early!" she said lightly. "Luckily, we're ready." She handed the baby to Zac and grabbed the diaper bag from beside the front door.

When Libby had shut the door behind her,

Zac said, "We need to get the car seat out of your car, right?"

Libby's eyes widened. "As a matter of fact, we do. What made you think of that?"

"Oh, it was mentioned in an article I read somewhere." Yeah, in the copies of *Modern Baby* that Hannah gave him. He'd found himself reading them late one night and, to his utter amazement, actually thought them interesting.

He watched Libby as she opened her car door and unfastened the infant seat. She wore the pink sundress she'd worn at the Lamaze class reunion, and all Zac could think about was getting his teeth on that obnoxious gold button.

After a long night and day spent making love with her, Zac wouldn't have thought he'd have enough energy to do it again so soon. He was only now beginning to realize that it would take a lot more than that to get enough of her. If such a thing were even possible. As a matter of fact, it would take a lifetime.

Whoa! Zac stopped dead. He didn't just want her in his bed. He wanted her in his life. He wanted to wake up with her, come home to her, go to sleep with her in his arms.

But his plans. His plans didn't have room for that. Not yet. He'd vowed to make the Fortune 500 by the time he was thirty-five. Four years to go. And until he'd met that goal, his work would require all his time and emotional energy. He wouldn't have any left over for a family. Why couldn't they have met five years from now?

"Zac? Is something wrong?"

"Uh, no. No, everything's fine," Zac mumbled and fastened the car seat in his car.

Libby was quiet on the way to Zac's, seemingly preoccupied with her thoughts. That suited Zac fine. He was still wrestling with thoughts of his own. He knew Libby was looking for a husband and father. She might be willing to take on Zac, but it wouldn't take too many weeks of his Saturday meetings and working until nine or ten before she would begin feeling resentful. Or, worse, maybe she'd feel lonely and neglected.

So why, how, had he allowed things to get this far? Someone was going to get hurt. And he had a horrible feeling that it wouldn't be only her.

The silence in the car had grown almost oppressive by the time they arrived at Zac's condo. The only one who didn't notice anything different was Victoria, who had fallen asleep by the time Zac had driven a couple of blocks.

"Can I help you with anything?" Libby asked as soon as they walked in the door.

"No. It'll take me only a couple of minutes to nuke the potatoes while I toss the steaks under the broiler. Why don't you go in the living room and make yourself comfortable? I'll be in there in a minute."

Libby saw the flowers as soon as she walked in the other room. "Beautiful flowers," she called out. "From one of your many admirers?"

"No." Zac came into the room. "From one of yours."

"One of mine?"

"They're for you."

Libby fell silent for a moment, then, inexplicably, her eyes filled with tears. "They're beautiful, Zac. Thank you," she said softly as she reached out and touched a soft rose petal with her finger.

"Uh, when you're ready to put Victoria down, you can use the second bedroom. It's across the hall from mine. I fixed the bed for her. I piled pillows all around so it's sort of like a nest."

She nodded and turned her head to blink the moisture away. This was harder than she'd thought. Every minute they spent together was one more memory she'd have to keep her warm all the long years ahead. Or to haunt her every moment. For her sake, for her own sanity, she was going to have to put an end to things. A heart could be broken more than once, and her heart would break every time she watched a science fiction movie or ate Italian food and he wasn't there. And the more memories they built together, the more memories would break her heart in the years to come.

But she'd take this night, this one night, and make one more memory. Just one more.

The steaks were grilled to perfection. The baked potatoes were hot and fluffy and sweet with melted butter. Libby scarcely managed a mouthful of each. She spent most of her time rearranging the food on her plate. Zac wasn't faring much better, she decided when she took a look at his plate. Most of his dinner, too, was untouched.

Zac stacked the plates in the sink without commenting on the mountains of food still left. They wound up sitting on the sofa, listening to music on Zac's compact disc player and staring at the tropical fish in their glistening aquatic world. Libby knelt in front of the tank and pointed to the two black and white angelfish. "What did you say these were named?"

"Michael and Gabriel."

Two angel's names. Just a few days earlier he'd acted horrified at the idea that he'd do something as sentimental as naming his fish. Maybe knowing her had changed him a little. It was only fair. Knowing him had changed her a lot.

She noticed a few other changes too. The plants had been rearranged on the mantel and were no longer lined up in a neat little row. Instead, they were grouped in less formal but more pleasing arrangements. The carefully arranged magazines on the coffee table had simply been stacked one on top of the other. And the toe of a tennis shoe poked out from under the edge of the sofa. She wanted to smile at that, but couldn't seem to make the corners of her mouth curl up.

Zac came and knelt beside her. Without looking at him she said, "It seems kind of silly to me to have fish coordinated with your living room." She pointed at the black mollies. "What did you say these were called?"

"They're black mollies. That's A, E, I, O, and U."

Libby couldn't resist a little smile at that. "That covers only five of them, and you've got six."

"The sixth one is Sometimes Y."

Libby turned to Zac. "I'm glad you named your fish."

He shrugged. "What else could I do? You even name your plants."

"How'd you know that?"

"Because I heard you mumbling to one this

morning, promising to water it later. Which one is Elliot anyway?"

"The spider plant hanging over the kitchen sink."

"Spider plant . . . Anyway, I didn't stand a chance. You would have named my fish for me, so I decided I'd better come up with names I could live with before you came up with Priscilla, Harry, and Bartholomew."

"I would never have come up with names like those. These are tetras, right? Did you name them too?"

"Libby," Zac murmured softly. "How much longer are we going to talk about my fish?"

"I don't know."

"Let's talk about something else." He reached out and grasped a handful of her hair, bringing it up to rub back and forth across his lips.

"What, um, what do you want to talk about?" she said faintly. He was now rubbing the strands of hair across her lips.

He released her hair and ran his knuckles down her cheek. "Oh, I don't know." He leaned closer and followed the path his hand had taken with his mouth. "I'd like to talk about you and me and this nice thick white carpet we're kneeling on," he said.

Libby could feel his warm breath against the

skin of her neck as he spoke. "What about the carpet?" Her voice was fainter still.

"It's soft." He pushed her gently down onto the plush surface. "Isn't it?"

"Yes," she breathed.

"And you're soft." He left a row of nibbling kisses along the top edge of her sundress. "And I need you more than you'll ever know."

"I need you too."

"That's good." His hands molded the soft fabric of the dress to her breasts. "This dress is indecent. Did you know that?"

"How?"

"This button," he muttered, his lips against the offending object. "This button dares a man to undo it."

"So why don't you?"

He raised his head and a slow, wicked grin spread over his face. "I intend to," he vowed huskily. He bent his head again and tugged on the button with his teeth. It came off easily, as if it had been sewn on with the express purpose of inciting a man to do this.

His hands smoothed the snug bodice down to her waist, baring her breasts. He cupped them lovingly in his hands, then ran his tongue around one rosy nipple, inviting it to pucker. He turned his attention to the other. "How does the baby nurse," he murmured against her breast. "Does she do it like this?" He took one swollen bud into his mouth and suckled.

Libby moaned. "Yes. No. It doesn't feel like this. It's like . . . you're . . . I . . ." Her words trailed off to an incoherent mumble.

"Sweet. You taste sweet." Those were the last words spoken by either of them, except for murmured words of passion, of love. There was a dark, desperate edge to their lovemaking that served only to heighten the sensations. Every feeling was explored to the fullest, as if each were aware this might be the last time.

Zac caressed Libby until she writhed with need, only to have her return the favor. They sought the pinnacle of fulfillment again and again, until they were both exhausted. They dozed, awoke sprawled on the carpet, and made their drowsy way down the hall to Zac's bed, where they loved one more time and fell asleep in each other's arms.

When Zac awoke it was early, just after dawn. He lay with Libby cuddled next to him and watched the rays of sun wink on one at a time. The sun seemed to love Libby. It caressed the creamy satin skin and danced over the sleek dark hair. He didn't think he'd ever seen anything lovelier than Libby in the morning. Unless it was Libby at night.

The night seemed to love her too. The dark flirted with the shadows in her hair and complimented her midnight-blue eyes. There wasn't a single time of day that didn't love her, he thought. And he loved her too. Loved her enough to realize that he couldn't give her what she needed. What she deserved. He loved her enough to let her go.

He heard soft babbling noises from the other room. He tugged on jeans and went in to check on the baby. She was wide awake and lying on her back, waving her arms in the air. He remembered seeing her on her stomach the night before and felt a distinct stab of pride that she'd apparently rolled over by herself. He dug in the diaper bag and came up with a fresh diaper, then changed her clothes too, dressing her in a frilly yellow shirt and matching pants. He carried her to the bedroom, where Libby still lay sleeping peacefully.

It hurt to see her sleeping in his bed. He didn't think he'd ever be able to sleep there again without thinking of her—the feel of her hair beneath his cheek, her soft honeysuckle scent, her arms and legs entwined with his.

She lay on her side, so Zac gently moved her arm out of the way and lay the baby next to her. It didn't take Victoria more than a second or two to find breakfast, and she suckled hungrily. Zac lay propped on one arm, watching, and felt the unaccustomed sting of tears in his eyes. It was such a gentle, natural, homey scene, and he felt a stab of loneliness to know he wouldn't be a part of their futures.

He wondered what kind of little girl Victoria would grow up to be? Would she wear her hair in a long ponytail? Would she like dolls or trucks? Teddy bears or tree houses? Maybe she'd like both. There was no law that said she couldn't. Would Libby make sure that Victoria had blocks to build with? He'd read that it improved hand-eye coordination. Would Libby—Zac stopped. It wasn't his concern. Would never be his concern.

Libby stirred and her eyelids fluttered once, twice, then opened. She looked down at the baby nursing contentedly at her breast, then up at Zac's dark, brooding gaze watching the two of them. A wave of shyness swept over her, and she looked back down at Victoria. They both lay in silence until Victoria had finished nursing and Libby sat up, laying the baby against her shoulder and patting her back.

As soon as she'd burped, Libby laid her down on the bed and turned to Zac. "We, um, we need to talk."

Zac sat up and swung his feet out of bed. "You're right, we do," he agreed flatly. "I'll wait for you in the living room."

ELEVEN

Libby wrapped a sheet around her and walked stiffly to the living room, grabbed her dress and panties from the carpet, and walked back to the bedroom. She dressed quickly, though the button from her dress was gone. A safety pin, found on Zac's dresser, fastened the strap around her neck.

From the shuttered look on Zac's face it was obvious that he either knew what she was going to say or had something equally bad to tell her. Libby picked up Victoria and cuddled her, needing the closeness. The baby's tiny, soft body and fresh, sweet smell gave Libby the strength to do what she had to do. She had to end this now. Victoria deserved more than the part-time attentions of her mother's part-time lover. She deserved nothing less than the full-time attentions of a full-time daddy.

Libby took a deep breath, then another, and walked back into the living room. As soon as he saw her, Zac spoke. "Libby, I don't have time right now for anything more than a casual relationship. And you deserve more than that. You and Victoria deserve—-"

"You're right." She looked down at the cooing baby in her lap. "I need someone who can be there. Not just for me, but for Cupcake too." She bit her lip and willed the tears stinging her eyes not to fall. "And I know that someone can't be you." Despite her determination not to cry, a single tear squeezed out from the corner of her eye and left a silver trail down her cheek.

"I can't be there all the time, but we could— we could continue to see each other—"

Libby looked up then, her eyes sparkling with tears and with fire. "No! I can't waste any more time with this. I need a man who's not afraid to commit himself."

Stung, Zac snapped back. "What do you mean afraid? I'm not afraid."

Libby leaned forward and looked him straight in the eye. "Aren't you? All this talk of time and plans—those are nothing but excuses. Your precious plans aren't engraved in stone, Zac. They're not even written in blood. Plans can be changed if you're not afraid. But you are afraid."

"Libby, I really lo—care about you."

Libby sighed and stood, walking to the big picture window overlooking Rockspring Park. "You probably do. *Care* is such a nice, insipid little word. It's a great word for someone who's afraid to commit himself any other way. But I want a man who loves me to distraction and one who's willing to love Victoria too. She and I both deserve as much."

Zac walked over to stand beside her. "Libby, I wish you could understand. My whole life I've lived by plans. They've never let me down. They've given me goals to attain. And I've got a hell of a lot I need to do in my life before I'll have the time to devote to a wife and family. It wouldn't be fair to any woman to ask her to put up with a man who can't give a hundred percent right now."

"You're right. It's not fair. I want more. And to get it, I'm going to have to get on with my life." She turned to look at him, more tears trailing down her cheeks. She let her eyes roam over his face one more time, as if memorizing each line, each contour, so she could recreate it during the long, dark nights ahead when she couldn't sleep and it hurt too much to cry.

"God, Libby," he murmured, and reached out a hand to touch her hair. He dropped it when she stepped away. "You don't know how much I wish I could give you what you need."

A poignant, wistful smile touched her lips. "And you don't know how much I wish that you cared enough to."

"It's not a matter of caring enough—"

"Isn't it? I love you, Zac. I love you enough to rearrange my life for you. You just can't bear the thought of rearranging your life for me. I understand. Really, I do. A wife and ready-made family is a lot for someone to take on. But there are men out there who aren't afraid." She turned away. "I need to go. May I use your phone to call a cab?"

"I'll take you home."

Libby shook her head. "I'd rather you didn't," she said calmly. "I'd really rather you didn't."

She didn't understand. He'd worked his whole life and he had certain goals. If he lost sight of those goals, then wouldn't his whole life have been a waste? "I'd like to see you home," he said again.

"I don't want you to. Now, may I use your phone?"

"If that's what you want, go ahead." He turned and stared back out the window. This wasn't in his plans. This ripping, slashing feeling in his gut. And as Libby hung up the phone and

hoisted the diaper bag, he felt the gash deepening.
"Let me help you with that."

"No, thank you," Libby said politely, then
opened the door and left.

He took an abortive step toward the door,
stopped, and slammed his fist against the wall.
Dammit! Dammit all to hell!

Teachers were due back at school in a couple
of weeks, and Libby couldn't wait. She couldn't
stand staying around her house anymore. The
past few days she'd taken the baby to the park,
to the museum—but not to the pre-Columbian
exhibit—even to a couple of matinee movies.
Anything was better than staying at home.

Nights weren't so easy, though. As darkness
fell, it brought with it thoughts and memories that
she didn't want. She wound up sleeping on the
sofa most nights. She'd go to bed, stare at the
ceiling, and think of lying in the same bed in Zac's
arms. It was too much. She'd grab her pillow and
head to the sofa, where she'd stare at the television
half the night. Too many more sleepless nights
and she wouldn't be fit to teach school.

Victoria seemed crankier than usual too. Libby
often wondered, as she walked the floor with the
fretful infant, whether the baby was responding to

Libby's own heartache or whether she missed Zac too.

Every time the phone rang, Libby's heart pounded and she nourished the irrational hope that it was Zac, telling her he was wrong and begging her to take him back. It never was, but that didn't stop her from hoping. Finally, she stopped answering the phone, letting her answering machine do it for her. She didn't feel like talking to anyone anyway.

"Libby darling, I called you a day or two ago, but maybe you didn't get the message. I'll call you later. Give my beautiful granddaughter a kiss. Bye."

"Sis? This is the third time I've called. Get the lead out, okay? I've got to tell you about the greatest guy. Oops, time for biology lab. See ya."

"This is Hannah. I know something happened between you and Zac. If it's any consolation, he looks miserable. If you want to talk, give me a call."

"Libby, it's Deb. I'm *not* leaving any more messages on this blasted machine! Pick up the damn phone and talk to me, girl. I've talked to Hannah and know something happened between you and Zac. No man is worth going into hibernation over and— Shoot. My next patient is due in five minutes. I'll call you tonight."

"Libby's, it's ah, Zac. You, ah, left a couple of the baby's things here. If you don't want to, ah, see me, I can leave them at the security desk downstairs. Libby, I really—well, I hope you're well. And the baby too."

Libby replayed that message at least a dozen times before she made herself erase it. God, I'm really losing it, she thought, and grabbed the baby, her purse, and her keys, and left. She couldn't stay around this big, empty place any longer. She was beginning to hate it.

Zac was beginning to hate his big, empty place. Every day he walked in from work, tossed his keys down, and began making excuses to go back out. He'd had dinner with every college buddy and business acquaintance he could dredge up. He'd played racquetball more in the past week than he'd played in the past two months combined. And he'd used the weight room downstairs more than he'd ever cared to. But anything was preferable to staying home alone.

Maybe he needed a few changes. It had nothing to do with Libby. He wanted to change the white carpet to some other color because he was tired of it, not because every time he walked into the room he pictured Libby and him entwined on it. He rearranged the bedroom, not because all he saw was Libby curled up in his bed, but because he wanted a change.

He even went out and bought a bright orange fantail goldfish and put it in his aquarium. Not because Libby said that a color-coordinated aquarium was silly, although it was. He did it because he wanted to.

The vase of flowers he'd bought for Libby still stood on the table, though most of the flowers were dropping their petals. He didn't know why he didn't throw them out. Maybe it was because they reminded him of Libby and all the reasons why it was better that they weren't involved. Oh, hell! Whom was he fooling? If it was better for anyone, it had to be her, because it sure wasn't better for him.

He wasn't sleeping worth a damn. When he did sleep, it only got worse. He had incredibly vivid dreams. Dreams of laughing and talking with her, which left him hating the silence when he woke up. Dreams of making love with her, which left him hot and heavy with need. Dreams of waking up to soft baby noises, which had him out of bed before he even realized there was no baby there.

Most nights he paced the floor until three or four in the morning. When loss of sleep left him too tired for early morning business meetings, he had his secretary postpone them all for a week or two. It was just as well, since he didn't seem to be able to think of anything but Libby for more than a few minutes at a time. He was in no shape to work at all.

Being home was worse, though. His condo used to be a safe, quiet haven. Now it seemed more like a shrine to Libby. He could see her sitting on the sofa, sipping her cup of tea, kneeling in front of his fish tank, sprawled naked on his carpet, curled up like a kitten in his bed. The silence he used to find so restful now roared with echoes of her voice, her laughter. Even the hard rock radio station he'd begun listening to didn't drown out the sounds.

So maybe her life was better, but his was going to hell in a handbasket.

"You look lousy."

"Thanks a lot, Hannah," Zac muttered dryly. "Just what I need to hear."

"I tell the truth. You've lost weight, the bags beneath your eyes look like they're waiting pickup at the local bus station." Her voice softened. "You look unhappy."

"I've been better," he admitted.

"Why don't you call her, Zac? I have it on the best authority that she's miserable too."

"I'm doing this *for* her. She wants a husband and a father for Victoria. I can't be either. Not yet. I've got too much I've planned to do."

"You made the plans, so why can't you change them?" Hannah asked baldly.

"It's not that simple."

"Yes, it is. You look at a family as a hindrance. Have you stopped to think they might be an advantage? They'd keep you centered. They'd give you something to work for. Let's say you reach whatever goal it is you've got for yourself. What good does it do? What do you have to show for it but a company—a building and a bunch of employees who all go home at night to their families. And you go home to what? An empty condo? A bunch of fake plants? A goldfish?" She stopped. "Hey, that *is* a goldfish. What's a goldfish doing in your aquarium?"

"It's a long story," he mumbled.

"Just think about what I've said, okay?"

"Hannah, I've been thinking about nothing else for the past two weeks. It's getting late. What time are you supposed to talk to Pritchard about your business license?"

"Oh, dear. I need to be there in fifteen minutes. Thanks for taking off work early to baby-sit Nicky for me. Are you sure you'll be okay?"

"I'll be fine."

After Hannah left, Zac sat on his sofa, holding his nephew on his lap. He found himself thinking about Victoria. She was a daintier baby than sturdy little Nick. Where Nick always seemed to be moving, kicking his legs, waving his arms, wiggling around, Victoria seemed to be content just to cuddle close.

He missed her. Nicky was growing up so fast. In the past few days he'd already cut two teeth. He wondered how Victoria had changed in two weeks. Before long she'd be chattering away and running around the house. And he wouldn't be there to see it. And if she ever said the word *da-da*, it wouldn't be to him.

He felt a knife stab in his gut at the thought. Then he took it one step further. If Libby ever said *I do*, it wouldn't be to him. *There*, *that twisted that knife but good*.

Nicky accidentally hit himself on the nose with the teething ring he was grasping and began to cry. Zac looked down and envied the baby's freedom to kick and scream. He'd like to do the same thing.

"Deb, I don't want to go out tonight," Libby protested tiredly. "I'm just not up to it."

"It's all arranged. Your mother said this guy

will be by to pick you up at seven. Who is he anyway?"

"Just a guy I knew in high school who's coming through town. Why Mom told him to drop in, I don't know. I'm going to be lousy company."

"I think it'll be good for you to get out and see that life goes on. You're letting this turn you into a hermit. Look at you. Your hair needs trimming, you've lost weight, and you look like you haven't slept in a month. This guy's gonna see you and report back to your mother that you look awful, and she'll be down here in a flash."

Libby sighed. "I know, I know. So what should I do?"

"Let me trim your hair, then we'll work on makeup to cover those circles beneath your eyes. And wear a really nice, sexy dress. It'll make you feel better. Trust me."

"Deb, I could always call and cancel."

"Go. Beats staying home tonight and crying, don't you think?" Deb said gently.

Libby shook her head. "Sometimes that's the only thing that helps."

Deb stayed and helped Libby with her hair and makeup. She dug through Libby's closet, holding up one dress after another, but Libby turned them all down. When Deb held up the white dress that Libby had worn to dinner with Zac, Libby blanched and tears filled her eyes, making it necessary to reapply her eye makeup.

Finally Deb pulled out a demure-looking silky pink dress. "Great color. Here, put this on."

Libby shook her head. "I don't want to wear that."

"I didn't ask you if you wanted to wear it. You don't want to wear anything I've pulled out so far. I'm telling you for your own good. Put this on. This guy will be here any minute and you're still running around in your bathrobe."

Libby didn't have the energy to argue, so she tossed her robe on the bed and slipped the dress over her head. "There. You satisfied?"

"Super. Turn around. Oops! We've got a problem here. It has no back."

"So."

"So that bra strap sure makes a statement."

"Without a bra, this dress'll make a statement."

"It'll be fine. I hear the doorbell." Deb went to answer the door and was back in a minute. "He's a knockout. And you don't look so bad yourself. You're right, though. Now that you've taken that bra off, that dress definitely says something. Anyway, Victoria and I are off to visit my mom. What time do you think you'll pick her up?"

"Early. Real early." Libby dawdled a few more minutes after Deb had left, not wanting to go out there, but she finally pasted on a bright smile and opened her bedroom door.

John Walker was tall and slim and looked like a California surfer. Most women would find him gorgeous, Libby thought. She, on the other hand, found she preferred her men tall, dark, and Zac.

She grabbed her purse and they walked out the door just in time to bump into Zac. Libby stared at him a moment before breathing. "Zac?"

Zac glared at the blond giant with a look of intense dislike, then pinned Libby to the door with his gaze. "Am I interrupting something?"

John slid a proprietary hand under Libby's elbow. "We were on our way out."

Zac looked directly at Libby, his eyes widening when he saw the fit of her dress. "You'll have to excuse us for a minute. We're on our way in." He took Libby's other arm and tugged her back inside the house, shutting the door in John's surprised face.

Libby jerked her arm out of his grasp. "What do you think you're doing?"

"You're not going out in that dress."

"I'll wear anything I want."

"You're not wearing that. You're not wearing a bra with it."

"I'm not going to discuss this with you. Zac, why did you come by?" Libby murmured.

Zac absently laid a hand on the head of Wells, who affectionately drooled on his pants leg. He looked at Libby a moment, noting the shadows beneath her eyes that even the skillfully applied makeup hadn't covered. She seemed a little thinner too, like him. And her eyes held the same haunting loneliness that he saw every morning in his own mirror. "Libby, I—I don't know. I just wanted to see you."

"I thought we decided we shouldn't see each other anymore."

"You decided it. I don't want to stop seeing you, baby."

The same need that coursed through her body every waking moment now vibrated in his voice. But need wasn't enough. She determinedly blinked back the tears that threatened. She'd already applied her makeup twice. She wasn't going to do it a third time. "Zac, this isn't going to—" She broke off at the urgent rapping on her front door. "We can't leave John just standing out there."

Zac strode over to the door, opened it, and said, "Excuse us." He shut the door again and turned back to Libby. "I want you."

"Wanting's not enough."

"You want me too."

She sighed and shook her head tiredly. "Zac, I'm not up to this."

"Admit it. You want me too."

"I don't have to admit anything."

Zac closed the distance between them in two steps. He pulled her up against him, his hands splayed over the bare skin of her back. He insinuated one leg between hers, knowing she couldn't help but notice his arousal. By her sharply indrawn breath, she had. "Do I need to prove it, Libby? Do I need to prove that you want me as much as I want you?"

He leaned back far enough to see the already achingly hard nipples displayed clearly by the clinging dress. "Then again, I don't have to prove it." He slid his hands around front and laid his palms over her breasts. "You did it for me."

Libby whirled away. "Fine. So I want you. That doesn't mean a thing. Because you can't give me what I want. No, not what I want, what I *need*."

Zac ran a hand through his hair. This wasn't going at all as he'd planned. But he couldn't think logically when he was around her. He couldn't think at all. All he could do was need. "Libby—"

"Would you please go? I have a date waiting."

Zac sighed in frustration. "Fine." He turned toward the door, then turned back. "One question, Libby, then I'll go."

She nodded.

"Do you still love me?"

A tear spilled down her cheek and she brushed at it, muttering, "There goes the makeup again." She looked up at Zac. "Suppose I do?"

"I need to hear it."

"Why?"

"I don't know!" he nearly shouted. "Damn, I don't know anything anymore. For God's sake, just say it!"

"Okay, then. Yes, I still love you." Another tear followed the first. "But it doesn't change anything."

Zac spun on his heel and stalked out the door, slamming it behind him, right in John's face yet a third time. He got halfway down the sidewalk, turned, and walked back up to the front door, banging on it with his fists.

When Libby flung the door open, John stepped up first. "Do you need some help, Libby?"

Zac snarled, "She doesn't need anything from you." He walked back into the house, dragging Libby with him, and slammed the door shut.

"I'm going to have to get a new door if you do that again," she said heatedly over the noise produced by the dog barking at the banging of the door.

"It changes everything." He ignored the pounding on the front door and turned to the dog. "Go." He pointed in the direction of the kitchen, and the dog wagged his tail and left.

"What are you talking about? What changes everything?"

"That you still love me. It changes everything."

"Zac," she choked out, "I can't keep going through this. It's tearing me up inside. You're tearing me up inside."

"Then we're even. You're tearing me up too," he whispered. "You've ripped my heart out and I'm dying inside without you." He reached out and ran his palm down her hair, then wrapped his hand in it. He tugged ever so gently and brought her closer. "My days are miserable, my nights are miserable. I need you there, Libby."

"This isn't fair," she whimpered. "I'm trying to do what's best, and you won't let me."

"What's best is you and me together." He released her hair, allowing his hand to slide over her shoulder, down her arm to her fingertips before dropping it to his side. They were standing only a few inches apart.

"What about Victoria?"

"And Victoria and the damned dog and even Elliot the spider plant."

"What're you saying?" Libby could hardly breathe as she waited for his answer.

There was another spate of pounding, and John shouted something about getting the police. Libby never took her eyes off Zac as she stepped to the door, cracked it, and said, "Sorry, John. Something's come up. Maybe next time." She shut the door again and repeated, "What're you saying?"

He took her hands in his. "That I love you. Will you marry me?"

"What about your plans?" Her voice was no more than a breathless squeak.

"They're my plans. I can change them if I want to. And I do want to. I need you in my life, baby, and if I have to marry the dog and the plant, I will."

"And the baby?"

"Funny thing. I kept waking up at night, listening for her, only she wasn't there. I missed her."

"She missed you too."

Zac bent his head to hers and, just before he took her lips, said, "And I missed her mother more than I can ever say. Say yes, baby. Please say yes." He moved his mouth over hers, seeking and finding his answer in the softening of her lips beneath his. He wrapped his arms around her and buried his face in her hair, holding her so close that they could feel each other's hearts beating.

"God, you feel so good next to me. I've been starving for your touch."

"Hold me closer, Zac." She wrapped her arms even more tightly around him.

"If we get any closer, we won't be able to breathe." He smiled into her hair.

"I don't care. Breathing is vastly overrated anyway."

"You're right. Who needs to breathe?" He lifted her clear off her feet and leaned her against the wall, pressing his body into hers. He kissed her again and again, and his hands seemed to be everywhere at once—caressing, molding, claiming.

He pulled her down to the floor, frantically pulling at their clothes, needing to be closer still. He knew he'd never get rid of the terrible sense of loneliness and loss he'd carried around until he'd buried himself in her. And only then after fifty years or so.

He murmured dark, primitive words of love and need as he filled her. He took with savage ruthlessness, giving no mercy. And he loved her with generosity, tenderness, and raw vulnerability.

It was a true bonding—physical and emotional—and when the sweet, fierce pleasure took over, they rode the waves together.

Afterward, he eased his weight to one side and raised up on an elbow. "I take it that meant yes?"

A slow, beautiful smile spread over her face, the smile he'd first noticed about her. The smile he'd fallen in love with.

"Yes."

"Is this all right?" Libby frowned at her reflection in the full-length mirror. "You don't think it's too much, do you?"

"No, the lace mantilla looks perfect with that dress. You look beautiful, so stop fidgeting."

"Is Zac here already?"

"He's downstairs with his brother."

"Um, did the caterer—?"

"Everything's perfect, Libby," Deb assured her. "Stop worrying."

Libby looked around the small room crowded with people she loved. Her mother, dressed in a blue lace suit, fussed over the bouquets of flowers that had just been delivered. Deb, Hannah, her younger sister, Faith, and Zac's sister-in-law Alice were all there, dressed in matching pink velvet and satin dresses.

"Are you sure you want to wear those shoes, dear?" her mother asked.

Libby looked down. "I'm sure. I know white sandals aren't exactly the norm for a December wedding, but I have my reasons."

The music started and they all filed downstairs, waiting in the foyer for their cue.

"Gracious," Deb said, eyes widening as she stared at the groom and best man through the doorway, "don't they look good?"

Libby peeked. "My word! I'm surprised half the women in church aren't swooning. I've never seen Zac in formal clothes before. I may make him wear them on the honeymoon."

"It's time."

Alice was first down the aisle, followed by Hannah, then Faith, then Deb. Then Libby stepped out.

"She's beautiful," Zac's brother, Matt, whispered to him. "Almost as beautiful as my Alice."

Zac didn't say anything at all. He had a lump in his throat the size of a grapefruit, and his eyes stung. He'd never seen anyone so beautiful in his life. The white satin gown she wore hugged her lush curves, and the lace mantilla floated behind her.

He smiled slightly when he noticed her bouquet—red sweetheart roses. Their gazes held for a moment and she smiled at him, then stopped by the front pew, where her mother sat, to give Cupcake a quick kiss. His eyes lingered a moment on his new almost-daughter. She looked like a cherub in a red velvet dress with white lace trim. And she was smiling and waving at him. He waved back, then turned to take Libby's hand.

She nudged his foot with her own, and he looked down, then nearly choked. She wore sexy white high-heeled sandals that showed off her bright red toenail polish to perfection. But the clincher was the little glittery heart she had glued on each toe.

The wedding passed in a haze. Zac didn't notice anything except Libby. He was conscious of every move she made, every breath she took, and finally he was conscious that she was really and truly his. And as he pulled her into his arms, he heard Victoria call out "Da." He jerked his head around and she smiled, lifted her arms, and said again "Da."

With unashamed tears in his eyes Zac strode down the aisle of the church with his beautiful new bride on one arm and his beautiful new daughter in the other.

THE EDITOR'S CORNER

It's summertime, and nothing makes the living as easy—and exciting—as knowing that next month six terrific LOVESWEPTs are coming your way. Whether you decide to take them to the beach or your backyard hammock, these novels, written by your favorite authors, are guaranteed to give you hours of sheer pleasure.

Lynne Bryant leads the line-up with **BELIEVING HEART**, LOVESWEPT #630—and one tall, dark, and dangerously handsome hero. Duke King is head of his family's oil company, a man nobody dares to cross, so the last thing he expects is to be shanghaied by a woman! Though Marnie MacBride knows it's reckless to rescue this mogul from a kidnapping attempt single-handedly, she has no choice but to save him. When she sails off with him in her boat, she fancies herself his protector; little does she know that under the magic of a moonlit sky, serious, responsible Duke will throw caution to the wind and, like a swashbuckling pirate, lay claim to the potent pleasures of her lips. Marnie makes Duke think of a seductive sea witch, a feisty Venus, and he's captivated by the sweet magic of her spirit. He wishes he could give her a happy ending to their adventure together, but he knows he can never be what she wants most. And Marnie finds she has to risk all to heal his secret pain, to teach his heart to believe in dreams once more. Lynne has written a beautiful, shimmering love story.

With **ALL FOR QUINN,** LOVESWEPT #631, Kay Hooper ends her *Men of Mysteries Past* series on an unforgettable note—and a truly memorable hero. You've seen Quinn in action in the previous three books of the series, and if you're like any red-blooded woman, you've already lost your heart to this green-eyed prince of thieves. Morgan West certainly has, and that lands her in a bit of a pickle, since Quinn's expected to rob the Mysteries Past exhibit of priceless jewelry at the museum she runs. But how could she help falling under his sensual spell? Quinn's an international outlaw with charm, wit, and intelligence who, in the nine and a half weeks since they have met, has stolen a necklace right off her neck, given her the mocking gift of a concubine ring, then turned up on her doorstep wounded and vulnerable, trusting her with his life. Even as she's being enticed beyond reason, Quinn is chancing a perilous plan that can cost him her love. Pick up a copy and treat yourself to Kay at her absolute best!

Ruth Owen made quite a splash when Einstein, the jive-talking, TV-shopping computer from her first LOVESWEPT, **MELTDOWN,** won a special WISH (Women in Search of a Hero) award from *Romantic Times.* Well, in **SMOOTH OPERATOR,** LOVESWEPT #632, Einstein is back, and this time he has a sister computer with a problem. PINK loves to gamble, you see, and this keeps Katrina Sheffield on her toes. She's in charge of these two super-intelligent machines, and as much as the independent beauty hates to admit it, she needs help containing PINK's vice. Only one person is good enough to involve in this situation—Jack Fagen, the security whiz they call the Terminator. He's a ruthless troubleshooter, the kind of man every mother warns her daughter about, and though Kat should know better, she can't deny that his heat brands her with wildfire. When it becomes obvious that someone is trying to destroy all she's worked for, she has no choice but to rely on Jack to prove her innocence. Superbly combining humor and sensuality, Ruth delivers a must-read.

STORMY WEATHER, LOVESWEPT #633, by Gail Douglas, is an apt description for the turbulent state Mitch Canfield finds himself in from the moment Tiffany Greer enters his life. Though she isn't wearing a sarong and lei when he first catches sight of her, he knows instantly who the pretty woman is. The native Hawaiian has come to Winnipeg in the winter to check out his family's farm for her company, but she's got all the wrong clothes and no idea how cold it can be. Though he doubts she'll last long in the chilly north, he can't help feeling possessive or imagining what it would be like to cuddle with her beside a raging fire—and ignite a few of his own. It seems he's spending half his time making serious promises to himself to keep his hands off her, and the other half breaking those promises. Tiffany wants to keep her mind on business, but she's soon distracted by the cool beauty of the land around her and exhilarated by Mitch's potent kisses. Then she runs into the impenetrable barrier of his mysterious hurt, and she knows she's facing the biggest challenge of her life—to convince Mitch that his arms are the only place she'll ever feel warm again. Gail's luminous writing is simply irresistible.

If intensity is what you've come to expect from a novel by Laura Taylor, then **HEARTBREAKER,** LOVESWEPT #634, will undoubtedly satisfy you. After an explosion renders Naval Intelligence officer Micah Holbrook sightless, he turns furious, hostile, desperate to seize control of his life—and also more magnificently handsome than ever, Bliss Rowland decides. Ever since he saved her life years ago, she's compared every other man she's ever met to him, and no one has measured up. Now that he's come to the island of St. Thomas to begin his recuperation under her care, the last thing she intends to allow is for him to surrender to his fear. It's hard fighting for a man who doesn't want to fight to get better, and the storm of emotions that engulfs them both threatens to destroy her soul. Unsure of his recovery, Micah keeps pushing her away, determined to ignore his hunger to caress her silken skin and the taste of longing on her lips. Knowing that only her passion can heal his pain, Bliss dares him to be conquered by his need. Laura will touch your heart with this stunning love story.

Last, but certainly not least, in the line-up is **CON MAN** by Maris Soule, LOVESWEPT #635. As head of a foundation that provides money for worthy causes, Kurt Jones is definitely no con man, but he knows that's how Micki Bradford will think of him once she learns of his deception. It all starts when, instead of letting his usual investigator check out a prospective grant recipient, he decides he'll try undercover work himself. He arranges a meeting with expert rider Micki, then on the pretense that he's interested in finding a stable for a horse, pumps her for information . . . even as his gaze caresses her and he longs to touch her as she's never been touched. He's tempted to tell her the truth, to promise he'll never hurt her, but Micki has learned the hard way how irresistible a good-looking liar can be. As Kurt sweeps her into a steamy charade to unearth the facts, Kurt vows he'd dare any danger to win Micki's trust, and teach her to have faith in his love. Maris does nothing less than thrill you with this exciting romance.

On sale this month from Bantam are two thrilling novels of passion and intrigue. First is **LADY VALIANT** by the magnificent Suzanne Robinson, whom *Romantic Times* has described as "an author with star quality." In this mesmerizing tale of grand romantic adventure, Thea Hunt is determined to repay the kindness of Mary, Queen of Scots, by journeying to Scotland to warn her away from a treacherous marriage. But in the thick of an English forest, she suddenly finds herself set upon by thieves . . . and chased down by a golden-haired highwayman who stills her struggles—and stirs her heart—with one penetrating glance from his fiery blue eyes. As a spy in Queen Elizabeth's service, Robin St. John is prepared to despise Thea, whom he considers a traitorous wench, to enjoy her torment as he spirits her away to a castle where she'll remain until Mary Stuart is safely wed. But he finds himself desiring her more than any other woman he's ever met. As captive and captor clash, Robin vows to use his every weapon to make Thea surrender to the raging fires of his need and the rising heat of her own passion.

Lois Wolfe returns with **MASK OF NIGHT,** a tantalizing historical romance where one bewitching actress finds love and danger waiting in the wings. Katie Henslowe's prayers are answered the night wealthy railroad tycoon Julian Gates becomes her benefactor, hiring her family's ragtag acting troupe for his new theater. But no sooner has her uncertain world begun to settle down than the potent kiss of a maddeningly attractive stranger sends her reeling. Matt Dennigan is arrogant, enigmatic, and broke—reasons enough for Katie to avoid him. And when, for secret motives of his own, the mysterious rancher begins to draw her into his search for evidence again Julian, Katie tries to resist. But in Matt's heated embrace she finds herself giving in to her innermost longings, only to discover that she and Matt are trapped in a treacherous quest for justice. Against all odds they become partners in a dangerous mission that will take them from a teeming city to the wild frontier, testing the limits of their courage and turning their fiercest desires into spellbinding love. . . .

Also on sale this month, in the hardcover edition from Doubleday, is **SATIN AND STEELE** by the ever-popular Fayrene Preston. Long out of print, this is a wonderfully evocative and uniquely contemporary love story. Skye Anderson knows the joy and wonder of love, as well as the pain of its tragic loss. She's carved a new life for herself at Dallas's Hayes Corporation, finding security in a cocoon of hardworking days and lonely nights. Then her company is taken over by the legendary corporate raider James Steele, and once again Skye must face the possibility of losing everything she cares about. When Steele enlists her aid in organizing the new corporation, she's determined to prove herself worthy of the challenge. But as they work together side by side, she can't deny that she feels more than a professional interest in her new boss—and that the feeling is mutual. Soon she'll have to decide whether to let go of her desire for Steele once and for all—or to risk everything for a second chance at love.

Happy reading!

With warmest wishes,

Nita Taublib

Associate Publisher

Don't miss these exciting books by your
favorite Bantam authors

On sale in June:
LADY VALIANT
by **Suzanne Robinson**

MASK OF NIGHT
by **Lois Wolfe**

And in hardcover from Doubleday
SATIN AND STEELE
by **Fayrene Preston**

From the bestselling author of
Lady Defiant, *Lady Hellfire*, and
Lady Gallant . . .

Suzanne Robinson

"An author with star
quality . . . spectacularly talented."
—*Romantic Times*

Lady Valiant

*Breathtakingly talented author Suzanne Robinson spins a
richly romantic new historical romance set during the spellbinding Elizabethan era. LADY VALIANT is the passionate love story of Rob Savage—highwayman, nobleman, and
master spy—and the fiery young beauty he kidnaps.*

A tantalizing glimpse follows . . .

Thea Hunt refused to ride in the coach. Heavy, cumbersome,
and slow, it jounced her so that she nearly vomited after a few
minutes inside it. She preferred riding at the head of her party,
just behind the outriders, in spite of Nan Hobby's objections.
Hobby rode in the coach and shouted at her charge whenever
she felt Thea was riding too fast.

"Miiiiiistress!"

Thea groaned and turned her mare. There was no use trying to ignore Hobby. It only made her shout louder. As the outriders entered the next valley, Thea pulled alongside the coach. The vehicle jolted over a log, causing Hobby to disappear in a flurry of skirts and petticoats.

"Aaaaoow," groaned Hobby. "Mistress, my bones, my bones."

"You could ride."

"That horrible mare you gave me can't be trusted."

"Not when you shriek at her and scare her into bolting."

"Aaaaow."

Thea pointed down the track that led into the oak-and-hazel-wooded valley. "We'll be following this road. No more spiny hills for a while."

She glanced up at the hills on either side of the valley. Steeply pitched like tent tops they posed a hazard to the wagons, loaded with chests and furniture, and to the coach. Yet she was glad to see them, for their presence meant northern England. Soon they would reach the border and Scotland. She heard the call of a lapwing in the distance and spotted a merlin overhead. The countryside seemed deserted except for their small party.

She'd insisted on taking as few servants and men-at-arms as necessary in order to travel quickly. She and Hobby were the only women and the men-at-arms numbered only seven including her steward. Still, the baggage and Hobby slowed them down, and she had need of haste.

The Queen of Scots was to marry that fool Darnley. When Grandmother told her the news, at first she hadn't believed it. Clever, beautiful, and softhearted, Her Majesty deserved better than that selfish toad. Thea had pondered long upon Grandmother's suggestion that she go to Scotland. Grandmother said Mary Stuart would listen to no criticism of Darnley, but that she might listen to Thea. After all, they had both shared quarters and tutors with the French royal children.

Thea had been honored with Mary's friendship, for both found themselves foreigners among a clutch of French children. Later, when Thea had need of much more than friendship, Mary had given her aid, had seen to it that Thea was allowed to go home.

Slapping her riding crop on her leg, Thea muttered to herself. "Don't think of it. That time is over. You'll go to Scotland for a time and then return to the country where no one can hurt you."

Nudging her mare, she resumed her place near the front of the line of horses and wagons. Only a cause of great moment could have forced her to leave her seclusion. She'd made her own life far away from any young noblemen. Some called her a hermit. Some accused her of false pride. None suspected the mortal wound she nursed in secret—a wound so grievous and humiliating it had sent her flying from the French court determined to quit the society of the highborn forever.

Her steward interrupted her thoughts. "Mistress, it's close to midday. Shall I look for a place to stop?"

She nodded and the man trotted ahead. Hunger had crept up on her unnoticed, and she tugged at the collar of her riding gown. Her finger caught the edge of one of the gold buttons that ran down the garment, and she felt a sting. Grimacing, she looked at her forefinger. Blood beaded up in a small cut on the side. She sucked the wound and vowed to demand that Hobby remove the buttons. They'd been a gift from Grandmother, but one of them had a sharp edge that needed filing.

It was a good excuse to replace them with the old, plainer buttons she preferred. These were too ornate for her taste. She always felt she should be wearing brocade or velvet with them, and a riding hat, which she detested. Only this morning Hobby had tried to convince her to wear one of those silly jeweled and feathered contrivances on her head. Refusing, she'd stuffed her thick black hair into a net that kept the straight locks out of her way.

She examined her finger. It had stopped bleeding. Pulling her gloves from her belt, she drew them on and searched the path ahead for signs of the steward's return. As she looked past the first outrider, something dropped on the man from the overhanging branches like an enormous fruit with appendages. The second outrider dropped under the weight of another missile and at the same time she heard shouts and grunts from the man behind her.

"Aaaaow! Murder, murder!"

A giant attacked the coach, lumbering over to it and thrusting his arms inside. A scrawny man in a patched cloak toppled into her path as she turned her horse toward the coach. He sprang erect and pointed at her.

"Here, Robin!"

She looked in the direction of the man's gaze and saw a black stallion wheel, his great bulk easily controlled by a golden-haired man who seemed a part of the animal. The stallion and his rider jumped into motion, hooves tearing the earth, the man's long body aligning itself over the horse's neck. Stilled by fright, she watched him control the animal with a strength that seemed to rival that of the stallion.

The brief stillness vanished as she understood that the man who was more stallion than human was coming for her. Fear lanced through her. She kicked her mare hard and sprang away, racing down the path through the trees. Riding sidesaddle, she had a precarious perch, but she tapped her mare with the crop, knowing that the risk of capture by a highwayman outweighed the risk of a fall. Her heart pounding with the hoofbeats of her mare, she fled.

The path twisted to the right and she nearly lost her seat as she rounded the turn. Righting herself, she felt the mare stretch her legs out and saw that the way had straightened. She leaned over her horse, not daring to look behind and lose her balance. Thus she only heard the thunder of hooves and felt the spray of dirt as the stallion caught up. The animal's black head appeared, and she kicked her mare in desperation.

A gloved hand appeared, then a golden head. An arm snaked out and encircled her waist. Thea sailed out of the saddle and landed in front of the highwayman. Terror gave her strength. She wriggled and pounded the imprisoning arm.

"None of that, beastly papist gentry mort."

Understanding little of this, caring not at all, Thea wriggled harder and managed to twist so that she could bite the highwayman's arm. She was rewarded with a howl. Twisting again, she bit the hand that snatched at her hair and thrust herself out of the saddle as the stallion was slowing to a trot.

She landed on her side, rolled, and scrambled to her feet. Ahead she could see her mare walking down the trail in search of grass. Sprinting for the animal, she felt her hair come loose from its net and sail out behind her. Only a few yards and she might escape on the mare.

Too late she heard the stallion. She glanced over her shoulder to see a scowling face. She gave a little yelp as a long, lean body sailed at her. She turned to leap out of range, but the highwayman landed on her. The force of his weight jolted the air from her lungs and she fell. The ground jumped at her face. Her head banged against something. There was a moment of sharp pain and the feeling of smothering before she lost her senses altogether.

Her next thought wasn't quite a thought, for in truth there was room in her mind for little more than feeling. Her head ached. She was queasy and she couldn't summon the strength to open her eyes. She could feel her face because someone had laid a palm against her cheek. She could feel her hand, because someone was holding it.

"Wake you, my prize. I've no winding sheet to wrap you in if you die."

The words were harsh. It was the voice of thievery and rampage, the voice of a masterless man, a highwayman. Her eyes flew open at the thought and met the sun. No, not the sun, bright light filtered through a mane of long, roughly cut tresses. She shifted her gaze to the man's face and saw his lips curve into a smile of combined satisfaction and derision. She could only lie on the ground and blink at him, waiting.

He leaned toward her and she shrank away. Glaring at her, he held her so that she couldn't retreat. He came close, and she was about to scream when he touched the neck of her gown. The feel of his gloved hand on her throat took her voice from her. She began to shake. An evil smile appeared upon his lips, then she felt a tightening of her collar and a rip. She found her voice and screamed as he tore the top button from her gown. Flailing at him weakly, she drew breath to scream again, but he clamped a hand over her mouth.

"Do you want me to stuff my gloves into your mouth?"

She stared at him, trapped by his grip and the malice in his dark blue eyes.

"Do you?"

She shook her head.

"Then keep quiet."

He removed his hand and she squeezed her eyes shut, expecting him to resume his attack. When nothing happened, she peeped at him from beneath her lashes. He was regarding her with a contemptuous look, but soon transferred his gaze to the button in his palm. He pressed it between his fingers, frowned at it, then shoved it into a pouch at his belt.

"I'll have the rest of them later," he said.

Reaching for her, he stopped when she shrank from him. He hesitated, then grinned at her.

"Sit you up by yourself then."

Still waiting for him to pounce on her, she moved her arms, but when she tried to shove herself erect, she found them useless. He snorted. Gathering her in his arms, he raised her to a sitting position. She winced at the pain in her head. His hand came up to cradle her cheek and she moaned.

"If you puke on me I'll tie you face down on your horse for the ride home."

Fear gave way to anger. In spite of her pain, she shoved at his chest. To her chagrin, what she thought were mortal blows turned out to be taps.

"Aaaow! Look what you've done to my lady."

"Get you gone, you old cow. She's well and will remain so, for now. Stubb, put the maid on a horse and let's fly. No sense waiting here for company any longer."

Thea opened her eyes. The highwayman was issuing orders to his ruffians. From her position she could see the day's growth of beard on his chin and the tense cords of muscle in his neck.

"My—my men."

"Will have a long walk," he snapped.

"Leave us," she whispered, trying to sit up. "You have your booty."

The highwayman moved abruptly to kneel in front of her. Taking her by the shoulders, he pulled her so that they faced each other eye to eye.

"But Mistress Hunt, you are the booty. All the rest is fortune's addition."

"But—"

He ignored her. Standing quickly, he picked her up. Made dizzy by the sudden change, she allowed her head to drop to his shoulder. She could smell the leather of his jerkin and feel the soft cambric of his shirt. An outlaw who wore cambric shirts.

She was transferred to the arms of another ruffian, a wiry man no taller than she with a crooked nose and a belligerent expression. Her captor mounted the black stallion again and reached down.

"Give her to me."

Lifted in front of the highwayman, she was settled in his lap a great distance from the ground. The stallion danced sideways and his master put a steadying hand on the animal's neck. The stallion calmed at once.

"Now, Mistress Hunt, shall I tie your hands, or will you behave? I got no patience for foolish gentry morts who don't know better than to try outrunning horses."

Anger got the better of her. "You may be sure the next time I leave I'll take your horse."

"God's blood, woman. You take him, and I'll give you the whipping you've asked for."

His hand touched a whip tied to his saddle and she believed him. She screamed and began to struggle.

"Cease your nattering, woman."

He fastened his hand over her mouth again. His free arm wrapped around her waist. Squeezing her against his hard body, he stifled her cries. When she went limp from lack of air, he released her.

"Any more yowling and I'll gag you."

Grabbing her by the shoulders, he drew her close so that she was forced to look into his eyes. Transfixed by their scornful beauty, she remained silent.

"What say you?" he asked. "Shall I finish what I began and take all your buttons?"

Hardly able to draw breath, she hadn't the strength to move her lips.

"Answer, woman. Will you ride quietly, or fight beneath me on the ground again?"

"R—ride."

Chuckling he turned her around so that her back was to his chest and called to his men. The outlaw called Stubb rode up leading a horse carrying Hobby, and Thea twisted her head around to see if her maid fared well.

"Look here, Rob Savage," Stubb said. "If you want to scrap with the gentry mort all day, I'm going on. No telling when someone else is going to come along, and I'm not keen on another fight this day."

"Give me a strap then."

A strap. He was going to beat her. Thea gasped and rammed her elbow into Rob's stomach. She writhed and twisted, trying to escape the first blow from the lash. Rob finally trapped her by fastening his arms about her and holding her arms to her body.

"Quick, Stubb, tie her hands with the strap."

Subsiding, Thea bit her lower lip. Her struggles had been for naught. Rob's arm left her, but he shook her by the shoulders.

"Now be quiet or I'll tie you to a pack horse."

"Aaaow! Savage, Robin Savage, the highwayman. God preserve us. We're lost, lost. Oh, mistress, it's Robin Savage. He's killed hundreds of innocent souls. He kills babes and ravages their mothers and steals food from children and burns churches and dismembers clergymen and—"

Thea felt her body grow cold and heavy at the same time. She turned and glanced up at the man who held her. He was frowning at the hysterical Hobby. Suddenly he looked down at her. One of his brows lifted and he smiled slowly.

"A body's got to have a calling."

"You—you've done these things?"

"Now how's a man to remember every little trespass and sin, especially a man as busy as me?"

He grinned at her, lifted a hand to his men, and kicked the stallion. Her head was thrown back against his chest. He steadied her with an arm around her waist, but she squirmed away from him. He ignored her efforts and pulled her close as the horse sprang into a gallop. She grasped his arm with her bound hands, trying to pry it loose to no avail. It was as much use for a snail to attempt to move a boulder.

The stallion leaped over a fallen sapling and she clutched at Savage's arm. Riding a small mare was a far less alarming experience than trying to keep her seat on this black giant. She would have to wait for a chance to escape, but escape she must.

This man was a villain with a price on his head. She remembered hearing of him now. He and his band roamed the highways of England doing murder and thievery at will. Savage would appear, relieve an honest nobleman or merchant of his wealth and vanish. No sheriff or constable could find him.

As they rode, Thea mastered her fears enough to begin to think. This man wanted more than just riches and rape. If he'd only wanted these things, he could have finished his attack when he'd begun it. And it wasn't as if she were tempting to men, a beauty worth keeping. She'd found that out long ago in France. And this Savage knew her name. The mystery calmed her somewhat. Again she twisted, daring a glance at him.

"Why have you abducted me?"

He gaped at her for a moment before returning his gaze to the road ahead. "For the same reason I take any woman. For using."

He slowed the stallion and turned off the road. Plunging into the forest, they left behind the men assigned to bring the coach and wagons. Several thieves went ahead, while Stubb and the rest followed their master. Thea summoned her courage to break the silence once more.

"Why else?"

"What?"

"It can't be the only reason, to, to . . ."

"Why not?"

"You know my name. You were looking for me, not for just anyone."

"Is that so?"

"Are you going to hold me for ransom? There are far richer prizes than me."

"Ransom. Now there's a right marvelous idea. Holding a woman for ransom's a pleasureful occupation."

As he leered down at her, fear returned. Her body shook. She swallowed and spoke faintly.

"No."

There was a sharp gasp of exasperation from Savage. "Don't you be telling me what I want."

"But you can't."

His gaze ran over her face and hair. The sight appeared to anger him, for he cursed and snarled at her.

"Don't you be telling me what I can do. God's blood, woman, I could throw you down and mount you right here."

She caught her lower lip between her teeth, frozen into her own horror by his threats. He snarled at her again and turned her away from him, holding her shoulders so that she couldn't face him. Though he used only the strength of his hands, it was enough to control her, which frightened her even more.

"I could do it," he said. "I might if you don't keep quiet. Mayhap being mounted a few times would shut you up."

Thea remained silent, not daring to anger him further. She had no experience of villains. This one had hurt her. He might hurt her worse. She must take him at his word, despite her suspicion that he'd planned to hold her for ransom. She must escape. She must escape with Hobby and find her men.

They rode for several hours through fells and dales, always heading south, deeper into England. She pondered hard upon how to escape as they traveled. Freeing herself from Savage was impossible. He was too strong and wary of her after her first attempt. She might request a stop to relieve herself, but the foul man might insist upon watching her. No, she would have to wait until they stopped for the night and hope he didn't tie her down.

Her gorge rose at the thought of what he might do once they stopped. She tried to stop her body from trembling, but failed. Her own helplessness frightened her and she struggled not to let tears fall. If she didn't escape, she would fight. It seemed to be her way, to keep fighting no matter how useless the struggle.

As dusk fell they crossed a meadow and climbed a rounded hill. At the top she had a view of the countryside. Before her stretched a great forest, its trees so thick she could see nothing but an ocean of leaves.

Savage led his men down the hillside and into the forest. As they entered, the sun faded into a twilight caused by the canopy of leaves about them. Savage rode on until the twilight had almost vanished. Halting in a clearing by a noisy stream, he lifted Thea down.

She'd been on the horse so long and the hours of fear had wearied her so much that her legs buckled under her. Savage caught her, his hands coming up under her arms, and she stumbled against him. Clutching her, he swore. She looked up at him to find him glaring at her again. She caught her breath, certain he would leap upon her.

His arms tightened about her, but he didn't throw her to the ground. Instead, he stared at her. Too confused at the moment to be afraid, she stared back. Long moments passed while they gazed at each other, studying, wary, untrusting.

When he too seemed caught in a web of reverie her fears gradually eased. Eyes of gentian blue met hers and she felt a stab of pain. To her surprise, looking at him had caused the pain. Until that moment she hadn't realized a man's mere appearance could delight to the point of pain.

It was her first long look at him free of terror. Not in all her years in the fabulous court of France had she seen such a man. Even his shoulders were muscled. They were wide in contrast to his hips and he was taller than any Frenchman. He topped any of his thievish minions and yet seemed unaware of the effect of his appearance. Despite his angelic coloring, however, he had the disposition of an adder. He was scowling at her, as if something had caught him unprepared and thus annoyed him. Wariness and fear rushed to the fore again.

"Golden eyes and jet black hair. Why did you have to be so—God's blood, woman." He thrust her away from him. "Never you mind. You were right anyway, little papist. I'm after ransom."

Bewildered, she remained where she was while he stalked away from her. He turned swiftly to point at her.

"Don't you think of running. If I have to chase you and

wrestle with you again, you'll pay in any way I find amusing." He marched off to shout ill-tempered orders at his men.

Hobby trotted up to her and began untying the leather strap that bound her hands. Thea stared at Robin Savage, frightened once more and eyeing his leather-clad figure. How could she have forgotten his cruelty and appetite simply because he had a lush, well-formed body and eyes that could kindle wet leaves? She watched him disappear into the trees at the edge of the clearing, and at last she was released from the bondage of his presence.

"He's mad," she said.

"Mad, of course, he's mad," Hobby said. "He's a thief and a murderer and a ravager."

"How could God create such a man, so—so pleasing to the eye and so evil of spirit?"

"Take no fantasy about this one, mistress. He's a foul villain who'd as soon slit your throat as spit on you."

"I know." Thea bent and whispered to Hobby. "Can you run fast and long? We must fly this night. Who knows what will happen to us once he's done settling his men."

"I can run."

"Good. I'll watch for my chance and you do as well." She looked around at the men caring for horses and making a fire. Stubb watched them as he unloaded saddlebags. "For now, I must find privacy."

Hobby pointed to a place at the edge of the clearing where bushes grew thick. They walked toward it unhindered. Hobby stopped at the edge of the clearing to guard Thea's retreat. Thea plunged into the trees looking for the thickest bushes. Thrusting a low-hanging branch aside, she rounded an oak tree. A tall form blocked her way. Before she could react, she was thrust against the tree, and a man's body pressed against hers.

Robin Savage held her fast, swearing at her. She cast a frightened glance at him, but he wasn't looking at her. He was absorbed in studying her lips. His anger had faded and his expression took on a somnolent turbulence. He leaned close and whispered in her ear, sending chills down her spine.

"Running away in spite of my warnings, little papist."

Thea felt a leg shove between her thighs. His chest pressed against her breasts, causing her to pant. He stared into her eyes and murmured.

"Naughty wench. Now I'll have to punish you."

Mask of Night
by
Lois Wolfe

author of *The Schemers*

A spectacular new historical romance that combines breath-taking intrigue and suspense with breathless passion.

She was an actress who made her living spinning dreams. He was a rancher turned spy whose dreams had all been bitterly broken. Against all odds, they became partners in a danger-ous mission that would take them from the teeming city to the wild frontier, testing the limits of their courage, and turning their fiercest desires into spellbinding love . . .

Read on for a taste of this unforgettable tale.

What use Gates might have for Katie was immediately apparent when Matt saw her emerge from the cloakroom in an understated emerald green gown. He made note of the dress, especially the top of it, the part that wasn't there. Nice swoop.

Real nice swoop.

Other men noticed too, as she crossed the lobby to the front desk. Matt debated following her. He was already late for dinner with the Senator, but, hell, a little more close observation couldn't hurt.

He joined her at the front desk. Her expression showed annoyance the moment she saw him, and he guessed she regret-ted trying to be polite to him.

"Looks like we both have business here," he said, leaning on the counter.

She turned her back on him, leaving him free to study her, the indignant thrust of her shoulders, the fragile trough of her spine. A wisp of dark golden hair had escaped its pin and rested in the curve of her neck.

"I'm here to meet my brother, Edmund Henslowe," she told the desk clerk.

The clerk went off to check the message boxes. She cocked her chin to her shoulder and sent Matt a withering look.

Hazel, he thought. Her eyes were hazel, more green than brown.

"Miss Katie Henslowe?" the clerk asked when he returned. "Mr. Henslowe wishes you to join him in his suite."

She was obviously startled. "His suite? Here?"

"Sixth floor. Number nineteen."

Six nineteen, Matt thought, looking ahead and not at her.

"Thank you." Icy, perfunctory. She was miffed.

The clerk had business at the other end of the long front desk, and they were alone for a moment.

She stood silent awhile, then turned to Matt. "Did you get all that?"

He was cautious. "What?"

"Don't play dumb. It looks too natural on you. Nice piece of news, wasn't it? The fact that my brother has a room here? Makes it seem like he has money, doesn't it? Well, let me assure you, you and whichever of our creditors you're the snoop for, Poppy does *not* have funds to make payments."

Matt played along, glancing around the opulent lobby. "This doesn't exactly look like a place for the destitute."

"I know." She backed down, stiffly. "Just, please, try to understand. My brother is here only to develop resources for the troupe. Now, I'm sure your loan department will be glad to hear that we may have the potential to resume quarterly payments." She paused. "You *are* a bank agent for Philadelphia Savings, aren't you?"

He shook his head.

"New York Fiduciary?"

"No."

"You work in the private sector, then, for an individual?"

"You could say that."

She looked away. "It's about Edmund, isn't it?"

"How'd you guess?"

Her glance took in his unfashionable attire and worn shoes. "My brother tends to attract an eclectic and, sometimes, illicit crowd."

"Which one am I? Eclectic or illicit?"

"You're a coward and a spy, and I doubt that you've got enough grapeshot in the bag to so much as fire off your name."

He looked at her for a long time. "Insults like that don't come from a lady."

"No." She held his gaze. "And they don't apply to a gentleman."

"Look, I'm not one of your brother's Jack Nasty lowlifes."

"You're not? And yet you have business here?" She studied him thoughtfully. "Are you meeting the senator then?"

Christ, how'd she know? He felt himself grow stony-faced, trying to keep reaction to a minimum.

"I remember," she went on, "seeing you waylay the distinguished senator backstage, Mr. . . . ?" She waited again for his name.

"Nasty," he said curtly. "Jack Nasty."

"I thought so."

To his surprise, she sidled close and put a hand on his arm. "Sir?" she called to the desk clerk. "My friend here has a request."

Matt tensed. What was she doing?

"Yes, sir?" the clerk asked, returning to them.

"He needs his messages," Katie interjected before Matt could speak.

"Of course." The clerk turned to Matt. "What is the name?"

Damn her.

She smiled prettily at him. "Now, come on. Don't dawdle," she said, as to a child. "You'll make us both late."

He hated being manipulated. He especially hated a woman who did it so well.

She patted his hand. "I know you've had a terrible sore throat." She turned to the clerk. "Maybe if you could just lean close, so he can whisper."

The clerk looked dubious, but obligingly leaned over the counter.

Matt felt pressure rise inside him like steam in a boiler.

"Still hurts?" she asked. "Would it be easier if you just spell it? I'm sure—"

"Dennigan!" The word shot out from between gritted teeth.

The clerk stared, astonished.

Katie removed her hand from his. "See how much better you sound when you try?" she said, then turned to the clerk. "Please check the message box for Mr. Dennigan."

Matt leaned close so no one would see him grab her wrist, grab it hard. "Dennigan," he repeated. "Matt Dennigan."

"Charmed, I'm sure."

She jerked her arm free as the clerk returned. His manner was noticeably more unctuous toward Matt. "Mr. Dennigan? It seems Senator Cahill is waiting dinner for you in the Walker Room."

"The Walker Room," Katie said. "Isn't that the salon for very private dining?"

The clerk nodded again. "Yes, ma'am. Right through the arch and turn left."

Katie looked at Matt. "Well, now, Matt, enjoy your dinner."

She was gracious in triumph, almost sweet, he thought, as she left him. She hurried to the elevator foyer. He stood a long while, watching until the accordion gate of the elevator collapsed sideways to let her on.

She had taken his amateurish game of sleuth and, in one polished play, raised the ante to life-or-death for the Senator's investigation. If she dared mention Matt Dennigan and Senator Cahill in the same breath to the cutthroat millionaire she was about to meet, the game was over. Julian Gates would run for cover and retaliate with all the congressional influence—and hired guns—his money could buy.

Jesus Christ.

OFFICIAL RULES

To enter the sweepstakes below carefully follow all instructions found elsewhere in this offer.

The **Winners Classic** will award prizes with the following approximate maximum values: 1 Grand Prize: $26,500 (or $25,000 cash alternate); 1 First Prize: $3,000; 5 Second Prizes: $400 each; 35 Third Prizes: $100 each; 1,000 Fourth Prizes: $7.50 each. Total maximum retail value of Winners Classic Sweepstakes is $42,500. Some presentations of this sweepstakes may contain individual entry numbers corresponding to one or more of the aforementioned prize levels. To determine the Winners, individual entry numbers will first be compared with the winning numbers preselected by computer. For winning numbers not returned, prizes will be awarded in random drawings from among all eligible entries received. Prize choices may be offered at various levels. If a winner chooses an automobile prize, all license and registration fees, taxes, destination charges, and other expenses not offered herein are the responsibility of the winner. If a winner chooses a trip, travel must be complete within one year from the time the prize is awarded. Minors must be accompanied by an adult. Travel companion(s) must also sign release of liability. Trips are subject to space and departure availability. Certain black-out dates may apply.

The following applies to the sweepstakes named above:

No purchase necessary. You can also enter the sweepstakes by sending your name and address to: P.O. Box 508, Gibbstown, N.J. 08027. Mail each entry separately. Sweepstakes begins 6/1/93. Entries must be received by 12/30/94. Not responsible for lost, late, damaged, misdirected, illegible or postage due mail. Mechanically reproduced entries are not eligible. All entries become property of the sponsor and will not be returned.

Prize Selection/Validations: Selection of winners will be conducted no later than 5:00 PM on January 28, 1995, by an independent judging organization whose decisions are final. Random drawings will be held at 1211 Avenue of the Americas, New York, N.Y. 10036. Entrants need not be present to win. Odds of winning are determined by total number of entries received. Circulation of this sweepstakes is estimated not to exceed 200 million. All prizes are guaranteed to be awarded and delivered to winners. Winners will be notified by mail and may be required to complete an affidavit of eligibility and release of liability which must be returned within 14 days of date on notification or alternate winners will be selected in a random drawing. Any prize notification letter or any prize returned to a participating sponsor, Bantam Doubleday Dell Publishing Group, Inc., its participating divisions or subsidiaries, or the independent judging organization as undeliverable will be awarded to an alternate winner. Prizes are not transferable. No substitution for prizes except as offered or as may be necessary due to unavailability, in which case a prize of equal or greater value will be awarded. Prizes will be awarded approximately 90 days after the drawing. All taxes are the sole responsibility of the winners. Entry constitutes permission (except where prohibited by law) to use winners' names, hometowns, and likenesses for publicity purposes without further or other compensation. Prizes won by minors will be awarded in the name of parent or legal guardian.

Participation: Sweepstakes open to residents of the United States and Canada, except for the province of Quebec. Sweepstakes sponsored by Bantam Doubleday Dell Publishing Group, Inc., (BDD), 1540 Broadway, New York, NY 10036. Versions of this sweepstakes with different graphics and prize choices will be offered in conjunction with various solicitations or promotions by different subsidiaries and divisions of BDD. Where applicable, winners will have their choice of any prize offered at level won. Employees of BDD, its divisions, subsidiaries, advertising agencies, independent judging organization, and their immediate family members are not eligible.

Canadian residents, in order to win, must first correctly answer a time limited arithmetical skill testing question. Void in Puerto Rico, Quebec and wherever prohibited or restricted by law. Subject to all federal, state, local and provincial laws and regulations. For a list of major prize winners (available after 1/29/95): send a self-addressed, stamped envelope entirely separate from your entry to: Sweepstakes Winners, P.O. Box 517, Gibbstown, NJ 08027. Requests must be received by 12/30/94. DO NOT SEND ANY OTHER CORRESPONDENCE TO THIS P.O. BOX.